# GOD,
## THE GRANDEST ILLUSION:
### THE BIRTH OF GOD FROM ALIEN/SUMERIAN WORSHIP

## DR. RON PLEUNE

God, The Grandest Illusion
Copyright © 2023 by Dr. Ron Pleune

All rights reserved. No part of this publication may be reproduced, distributed, or transmitted in any form or by any means, including photocopying, recording, or other electronic or mechanical methods, without the prior written permission of the author, except in the case of brief quotations embodied in critical reviews and certain other non-commercial uses permitted by copyright law.

ISBN
978-1-961250-77-2 (Paperback)
978-1-961250-78-9 (eBook)
978-1-961250-76-5 (Hardcover)

*GOD…THE GRANDEST ILLUSION*

*A Study and Guide of authentic facts regarding the extraterrestrial influence and Hebrew acceptance in creating a belief in a Judeo/Christian God and how-to live-in Peace without a God*

**By: Dr. Ron Pluene**

# Table of Contents

Chapter 1　Knowing That What You Accept Is the Real Truth .......1

Chapter 2　Finding the Real Truth ................................................. 19

Chapter 3　The Evidence of Our Ancestry ......................................50

Chapter 4　Biblical Issues ................................................................69

Chapter 5　Victorious Living without God ................................... 142

# Chapter 1

# Knowing That What You Accept Is the Real Truth

**Trick or Truth**

As we go through life from birth to death, we look at what is presented to us in life from many angles and ask a question, "With what I am about to experience, presently experiencing or will experience in the future, the real truth to the scenario of life?" Many times, that question is brought to our mind after a situation has passed and we are left to pick up the pieces of a broken life…or in positive situations, we ask, "Was this the way life was to benefit me?" "Did I have or was supposed to have made a different decision whereby the real truth of life and its consequences would have turned out different?"

Think back to situations in which something positive or something negative had happened, and you said to yourself, "If only I had done this or that…then the situation I am in would not have turned out the way it did." Within this context, we tend to bring in mitigating circumstances such as other people and events that bring us to the point of squeezing out of personal accountability.

Whether the outcome is positive or negative, we must deal with the "Real Truth." Religions, and particularly the Christian Religion, are full of dealing with supposedly "The Real Truth," even though people tend to butter it up, cut it up, or cover it up to avoid the inconvenience of responsibility and accountability.

Two of the most notable Christian teachers are deaf to The Real Truth of UFO, Evangelist Billy Graham, and Pope Francis.

Billy Graham stated in "Aliens Archives: Billy Graham Evangelistic Association," accessed February 18, 2019, https://billygraham.org/amswer/bible-say-anything-life- planets/, the "Bible does not say anything about UFO or the possibility of life on other planets."

Pope Francis was not as dogmatic and tactfully responded to the question regarding alien existence by stating, "Honestly, I wouldn't know how to answer," and then responded, "until America was discovered, we thought it didn't exist; and instead, it existed." The article was titled "Do Aliens Exist? Pope Francis Tackles This (and Other Things) in New Interview," October 15, 2015.

(https://www.catholicnewsagency.com/news/32820/do- aliens-exist-pope-francis-tackles-this-and-other-things-in- new-interview.)

The two situations above are a prime example of ignoring what is called "the Law of Rightness." "The law of rightness" is dictated by policy, terms, contract, etc., that states how things are supposed to function in initial formation as well as through the life of the item or function. The Law of Rightness demands a right response by those in a position of leadership of knowledge to proclaim the truth. Both Billy Graham and Pope Francis knew at the time of the interview that UFO sightings, photos, and abductions existed... and while one flat denied their possibility, the other one at least was open to the possibility of their existence.

This same law, the Law of Rightness, must be applied to the Christian Bible also. Many believe the Bible is complete, yet there are omissions, errors, and inconsistencies that exist and are dealt with later in this work.

Once again, the challenge for us today is to ensure that what we accept is the real truth, and if there is any doubt, be open-minded for future revelations.

## Inspiration/Mental Telepathy

In Biblical documentation, as is addressed in this writing, it is customarily held that revelation of information and the documentation of it was given by what is known as "God in audible terms or mental telepathy" as in Gen. 24:1 (KJV) and many other references, and is referred to in the New Testament as the "inspiration of God," II Timothy 3:16 (KJV), and is defined in Strong's Exhaustive Concordance of the Bible, Greek Dictionary of the New Testament, page 36, as being "divinity breathed," or as the Christian Community would say "God-breathed."[1]

One of the toughest approaches by a Christian, or other believers in God, is to be open-minded about other possibilities, discrepancies, and errors made by theorists, scribes, historians, etc., and be willing to examine the material without being biased or judgmental. After all, there is the distinct possibility of human error. Why? That is a hefty question that requires an open mind to the reality of history that can be explained as follows.

The Bible does not have all the answers to history! There are many instances where language such as "After these things…" in Genesis 15:1, "And it came to pass…" in Genesis 6:1 and 14:1 which leaves an undefined amount of time and conditions to be explained.

---

[1] Strong, LL.DLL. D, S.T.D. (1984. 36) *The New Strong's Exhaustive Concordance of the Bible.* Nashville, TN: Thomas Nelson, Inc.

*Dr. Ron Pleune*

The point here is that the Bible was written from a certain point of view, namely the observation of mankind through the eyes of an Old Testament writer even though it was by "...inspiration of God..." II Timothy 3:16 (KJV). All this statement means is that the God that was worshiped "motivated" someone to write what came through the eyes and ears of a person.

This leads us to examine the means or the method of "inspiration." This whole subject ties into what will be presented shortly of who God was at that time, but for now, we need to focus on how mankind received communication from God. This type of communication is no different than what many people receive as the telepathic transmission of sentences or thoughts from extraterrestrials that visit the earth and want to express information or give instructions. This is described and confirmed by Billy Meier's main teacher, Semjase, in Contact Report#2,#3, and#544.

Once again, I caution those that are believers in God to open their minds and take in some important information. The following information will prove that **God is none other than a high-ranking extraterrestrial that has immense knowledge and usage of powers and energy of the universe through technological advances that are beyond our imagination.** This is confirmed many times by the Plejaren in Contact Report #1, #5, #10, #32, #236, #427, #765, Asket's Explanations- Part 1- *Regarding the Danger of Religion*, (February 1953); article: *Faith (Belief) and God*, (January 2009), by Billy Eduard Meijer; *The Gods of the Earth Were Human*, OM 52:8, (January 12, 2005); *Who or What is God?*, Quote from an interview with Billy Meier (1998), and there are over 60 references in the *Goblet of the Truth* to the fact that there is no God, Gods or Godhead, including chapter 11 verse 8, as follows: "Truly, you have stories (fables) of the origination of your world and of the firmaments (universe, conceived through hazy pictures (delusions) of people of your kind (human beings) who thought-up gods and tin gods for themselves who are supposed to have created your earth, but these are in truth only fabulated narratives (myths) by imposters without sense and value, and everything is only evident deception (delusion), because truly everything persisting (existing) was set into existence (life) solely through the determining laws and recommendations of the primal power of all primal power (Creation)."

Going back to the phrase above, **God is none other than a high ranking extraterrestrial that has immense knowledge and usage of powers and energy of the universe through technological advances that are beyond our imagination;** we can now begin to understand how advanced Sumeria was as described in the "Kings List" and recorded in Cuneiform on clay tablets of how alien humans came to earth from the cosmos of the universe *"After the kingship descended from heaven, the kingship was in Eridug."* https://en.wikipedia.org/wiki/Sumerian_King_List.

In *History Begins at Sumer,* by Samuel Noah Kramer, he points out the "first advancements" in civilization through the technological guidance of the so-called Kings (human aliens) as follows.

---

1. The First Schools
2. The First Case of 'Apple Polishing'
3. The First Case of Juvenile Delinquency
4. The First 'War of Nerves'
5. The First Bicameral Congress
6. The First Historian
7. The First Case of Tax Reduction
8. The First 'Moses'
9. The First Legal Precedent
10. The First Pharmacopoeia
11. The First 'Farmer's Almanac'
12. The First Experiment in Shade-Tree Gardening

13. Man's First Cosmogony and Cosmology
14. The First Moral Ideals
15. The First 'Job'
16. The First Proverbs and Sayings
17. The First Animal Fables
18. The First Literary Debates
19. The First Biblical Parallels
20. The First 'Noah'
21. The First Tale of Resurrection
22. The First' St. George'
23. The First Case of Literary Borrowing
24. Man's First Heroic Age
25. The First Love Song
26. The First Library Catalogue
27. Man's First Golden Age
28. The First 'Sick' Society
29. The First Liturgic Laments
30. The First Messiahs
31. The First Long-Distance Champion
32. The First Literary Imagery
33. The First Sex Symbolism
34. The First Mater Dolorosa
35. The First Lullaby
36. The First Literary Portrait
37. The First Elegies
38. Labor's First Victory
39. The First Aquarium

Other "firsts" as pointed out by Joshua J. Mark, *Podcast*, October 9, 2019, are the invention of "dividing day and night into 12-hour periods, hours into 60 minutes, and minutes into 60 seconds, oldest heroic epic, monumental architecture, and irrigation techniques."

The so-called "Kings" that are identified on the "King List" were worshiped as "gods" because of their immense knowledge, skills, and wisdom in vast areas of living... which isn't much different than the god-culture we live in today with making icons of people in sports, movies, politics and other areas of social notoriety.

Based on this approach, it must be pointed out that those on the "King List" passed on in time just like those who seek and accomplish fame and fortune today through titles, trophies, and monetary gain, and asset holdings. And even though the Sumerians, including Abraham and his kin, were told to put away their idols, Joshua 24:2, 14, (KJV), the worship of the main idol-God in Sumerian history has continued through today in various Christian, Muslim, and Jewish faiths.

The accounts by the Plejaren are true and factual. They have been relayed to Billy Meier face to face by Plejaren people as well as by mental telepathy. One of the Plejaren people by the name of Ptaah states in *Contact Report #721*, line 39, on June 14, 2019,... since 389,000 years earlier other extraterrestrials had come to earth and had settled far and wide on all continents...".

So, it is acknowledged that various types of ET have visited and even lived, as well as mated, with earth humans. **The key to what history is true, fabricated in part, or distorted** is explained by Ptaah (one of Billy's ET contacts from the Planet Erra in the Pleiades) in the same Contact Report. Here is the extract of lines 73 through 76.

"73. Truthfully, the records were only written out many decades after the real events by scribes with their own interpretations, ideas, and fantasies, just as was the case with the six proclaimers.

74. In the case of Muhammad, for example, it was more than 100 years after his death before the first words were written about him, and his **teaching was completely disregarded and rewritten and replaced by a completely re-invented one.**

75. Hence, the true teaching that Muhammad brought, the 'teaching of the prophets,' i.e. 'teaching of the truth, the teaching of the spirit, the teaching of the life was not simply **falsified** beyond recognition, but it was, as was already the case with the same teaching of Jmmanuel, completely **denied and replaced by a new truth-falsified religious history that was fantasized** together from the ground up and directed towards a godhead and spread.

76. In addition, over the course of centuries, **new rules, rituals, prayer-, behavior-** and other regulations as well as **religious laws,** etc. were **invented over and over again**, which were fantasized in a conscienceless manner into the **irrationally- and confusingly-invented senseless religious teaching** and were mendaciously ascribed to the proclaimers Jmmanuel and Muhammad."

What makes the Contact Notes of Billy Meier so important?

1. They are from live humans from another planet.
2. They are accurate. (Dates, times, places, events, chemicals, people, etc.)
3. The Plejarens have been witnessed by many in Switzerland.
4. Ptaah has personally been seen by Billy's ex-wife in their home
5. Artifacts given to Billy by the Plejaren have been verified.
6. The general public has seen the Plejaren ships.
7. Even my wife and I have seen the Plejaren ships fly over, and one landed 300 ft. from me.

The truth is evident and gives assurance that the Chronology of Earth is true, which then verifies the Chronology of leadership of the Hebrews

*God, The Grandest Illusion*

and its truth in Contact Reports #236, #70, #5, #9, #38, and #39. A breakdown of this is below.

## The Chronology of Earth History (detailed)

This chart shows important moments in Earth history based on information from the Plejarens. Dates are only estimated to show the chronology of events.

- 22 Million B.C. The first Lyrans **came to Earth and colonized**.
- Red, Brown, and white peoples (**contact #236**)
- The brown (strongly dark-skinned) were established in Africa and spread to Australia and New Zealand, and other locations. (**contact #236, line 196**)
- 389,000 B.C. 144,207 Lyrans **came to Earth and settled here**, forever changing the genetics of Earthman.
- 228,000 B.C. A Lyran leader named Asael leads 360,000 Lyrans to a new home in the Pleiades.
- 226,000 B.C. Asael dies, and his daughter Plejara becomes the ruler. The system is now called the Plejara.
- 225,000 B.C. Plejara's scout ships discover Earth, and **colonies are founded here** and on **Mars and Milona**.
- 196,000 B.C. **War breaks out on Earth, and its people are evacuated to the Plejas**. Forty years later, Milona destroys itself and becomes the asteroid belt. Mars is thrown out of orbit, and all life is gone.
- 116,000 B.C. For the past 80,000 years, **several small colonies have been tried** by the Lyrans- mostly exiled criminals.
- 71,344 B.C. The Great Pyramids were built in Egypt, China, and South America by Lyrans.
- 58,000 B.C. The Great Plan. The Pleiadians **build a great society on Earth** that lasts for almost 10,000 years.

*Dr. Ron Pleune*

- 48,000 B.C. Ishwish **Pelegon (King of Wisdom-IHWH/God- contact #5)** comes to Earth and builds a wonderful society that lasts for around 10,000 years.
- (38,000 B.C. peace ended& none returned for 7,000 yrs.- contact #9)
- (Under leadership of an IHWH- contact #9)
- 31,000 B.C. **Atlantis is founded** by a man named Atlant, who comes with his people from the Barnard Star system.
- 30,500 B.C. The great city of **Mu was founded** by Muras, the father of Atlant's wife, Karyatide. His empire is sometimes called Lemuria.
- 30,000 B.C. The **black race** comes from Sirius.
- 16,000 B.C. **Arus is exiled from Earth** for trying to start wars. He hides out with his followers in the Beta Centauri star system.
- 14,000 B.C. **Arus (aka "the Barbarian" aka contact #9; aka Ashtar Sheran, line 3, Aruseak, line 11, and Arussem, line 19, per contact #38)) and his men return to Earth** and settle in Hyperborea, which is the current location of Florida (**contact #9**).
- 13,000 B.C. The scientist Semjasa, the second in command to **Arus (aka Ashtar Sheran, line 3, Aruseak, line 11, and Arussem, line 19, per contact #38)**, creates two Adams, who bear a child named Seth. This becomes the legend of Adam and Eve **(contact #9) (weaves lies and deceit into religious teachings, lines 19 thru 21- contact #38)**.
- (Takes 3 human races under his control via subleaders and guard angels. They are known today as "Indians," "fair-skinned inhabitants who had settled around the Black Sea; and the third were Gypsies along the south of the Mediterranean Sea, who were called Hebrews." (**Line 154, contact #39**). (Arus elevated himself above Creation itself as God, "imposed harsh and severe laws demanding the blood of the guilty"- his sub-leaders were assistant creators and Gods, (**line 156-158, contact #9**).
- 11,000 B.C. **Arus II attacks the Sumerians**, who
- flee into the mountains.
- 11,000 B.C. A group of ETs of unknown origin

- arrives, led by a leader named Viracocoha, who controlled the city of Tiahuanaco. His base was on an island named Mot. He provided the inhabitants of **Easter Island** the tools to build the strange statues there which represent him.
- 9,498 B.C. Atlantis and Mu destroy each other and ruin the planet. The air is not breathable for 50 years. All survivors are driven underground.
- 9,448 B. C. **Jehovan (called Jehovah in contact #38 and Jehavon in contact #70, line 136),** the third son of Arus XI, takes over the three remaining tribes left on Earth and becomes the ruler of (1) "Indians," (2) "fair-skinned inhabitants who had settled around the Black Sea (Armenians of today), and (3) the Hebrons, also known as the Hebranons **(contact #70, line 140)**
- **Kamagol the First** succeeded the "JHWH" Jehovah. The Gypsies along the south of the Mediterranean Sea, called Hebrews (Hebreons- distant relatives of the Israelis, **contact #136, all of part 2),** joined up with Kamagol **(contact #38, line 28).** "Forced earth humans into its power and completely lead them into a cultic religion confusion." **(contact #38, lines 30-31).**

"Created a center and headquarters deep under the surface of the pyramids of Giza" **(contact #38, lines 32-34).**

Later overthrown by Kamagol the Second

- 8,239 B. C. The Destroyer Comet passes closely by Earth and causes the Atlantic Ocean to part.
- **8,104 B.C. The Biblical Flood.**
- 6,000 B.C. Venus is pulled out of its orbit **around the planet Uranus** by the Destroyer Comet and is in orbit around the sun.
- 5,981 B.C. The Destroyer Comet comes close to Earth, causing great destruction. It also changes the orbit of Venus.

*Dr. Ron Pleune*

- 5,000 B.C. **Jehav, the son of Jehovan, takes over rulership**. Ruled wickedly, screamed for blood and revenge (contact #70, line 146).
- 4,930 B.C. The Destroyer Comet once again passes
- close by Earth, causing tidal waves of destruction.
- 3,660 B.C. **Jehovan, aka Jehovah aka Jehavon)** murdered by his only son Jehav (**contact #70, line 145**).
- 3,320 B.C. **Jehav rule ended (contact #70, line 146).** Had sired 3 sons, Arussem, Ptaah, and Salam. Arussem took control for a while until his two other brothers expelled him and put him in exile (**contact #70, line 149-150**). Arussem secretly returned to earth to Egypt below the Pyramids to lead earth humans in corrupted religious teachings. (**contact #70, lines 152-153**).
- 2080 B.C. **Karmagol the First replaced Jehova**, "forced all earthly religions into his control and created terrible cults which demanded human blood, which were able to be partially maintained until the present." (**contact 70, line 160**).
- Karmagol the Second replaced his father and carried out "monstrous mass murdering of earth- born terrestrial human beings, who he slapped under his religious power through many kinds of means." He died Dec. 27, 1976 (**contact 70, line 163-165**)
- 2080 B.C. **Jehova**, aka **Jehovan**; "old and weak, he was displaced, and his nephew Kamagl the First, took over the evil command of the Giza Intelligences" (**contact #70, line 159**).
- 1500 B.C. The Destroyer Comet passes by Earth, causing the Santorini Volcano to erupt. It also pulls Venus into its current orbit around the sun.
- 1320 B.C. Jehav is murdered by his son, Arussem, who has two sons named Salem and Ptaah.
- 1010 B.C. Arusseam is driven out of power by his sons and hides out under the Great Pyramid with his followers. They call themselves the Bafath.
- 32 A. D. Jmmanuel is crucified on a Y-shaped stake and survives.

- 1844 A.D. The initial phase of the "Golden Age," the transition phase of 184 years ( **"rapidly evolving events, discoveries, intentions, etc.- contact #9).**
- 1933 A.D. Aruseak; **aka Ashtar Sheran, line 3, Aruseak, line 11, and Arussem, line 19, per contact #38)** regained control from Kamagol (**contact #38, lines 40-47 and 60-63**). He left the Giza Intelligences and became autonomous but transmits messages to earth humans using telepathic impulses.
- 175 A.D. approx.- **Jehova**, aka **Jehovan**; The Biblical God, called "The Unjust and Cruel One," came to his end 2,150 years ago (from the contact year of 1975) (**contact #39, line 71**).
- 2028 A.D. Culmination of this period (**contact #9**).

<u>From contact #70, Thursday, January 6, 1977; information given by Billy Meier's main teacher, Semjase</u>

The knowledge of what has happened does nothing for us unless we learn what makes a person/people worship God. The following are factors that influence a person into following or worshiping a God today, just as various extraterrestrial influences had on people down through the millennia.

An identity with a God (i.e., friendship or co-workman)

The sense of serving a "greater cause."

The sense of reliance for safety, provisions, understanding, forgiveness, and direction

The sense of guidance for the present and future

The sense of a purpose for wanting to be "right."

The sense of being relieved from personal accountability by the forgiveness of a God

> The sense of assurance that heaven awaits after passing away

If this is the case, then the account of creation to those living at the time of the writing of Genesis had to have the knowledge of writing in the Hebrew language as well as the history of mankind from the time before mankind. The next question is, "who taught them the definitions, pronunciations, and applications of the words to adequately describe the events that took place?" Especially since we know that they did not have the exhaustive dictionaries that we have today.

The Christian would say that this was all the involvement of God in various ways. Yet there is a more reliable and fuller account of who the Hebrew people are and who God was that the Christian Church is blind to or refuses to acknowledge.

## Attitude

In my past years as a Christian in many churches, as a visitor or member, I never heard a sermon on ufology nor its relevance to the Bible, even though Ezekiel Chapter 1 (KJV) comes the closest to a UFO description. Later in life, as a church pastor and campground evangelist in private campgrounds, the topic of ufology and its involvement with Biblical events was never discussed. It was as if the subject was taboo, and it was to be left alone.

To be fair to those that do not believe in UFOs and to those that do, I write the following story of a deacon in a Baptist Church I used to attend in the north end of Grand Rapids, Michigan.

One day, in my late teens, I asked Harry S. about UFO. He claimed that it was "of the devil" and that they did not exist. I respected Harry very much; he was a hard-working family man with a wife and some children. He had been a Sunday School Teacher and, most notably, a deacon for at least 20 years. His answer seemed "final," and the matter was dropped. When I was released from the Navy in 1973, I went to see Harry S., who lived only a few blocks from where I grew up.

Harry invited me in and told me to sit down...he said that there was something inside him that told him he had to tell me. Harry S. relayed the story of how he and his wife went to the Upper Peninsula of Michigan to clean out a cottage that they had sold and decided that since it was so late at night, they would stop at the nearest motel/hotel on the way to Grand Rapids and stay the night.

A short while after they started on the road, they spoke to each other about some pulsating lights off in the distance on the drivers' side of their car. After a short while, the pulsating lights stopped, but then a few minutes later, a UFO of a saucer shape came up the road right at them and stopped in front of their car. The UFO turned on a red light and slowly hovered just above the car as it proceeded from the front to the back as if it were scanning the occupants in it. Harry S. stated that the UFO shut off all electricity in their auto and that the UFO returned to the front of the vehicle where it hovered, shut off its red scanning light, angled toward the sky, and shot off out of sight. After a short while, Harry S. reached over to the key and turned the car on. All seemed to operate fine, and he put the vehicle into drive and headed down the road.

Harry S. stated to me that after that incident, they didn't tell anyone of it, yet he said that he felt something inside told him that he had to tell me. Was he afraid of being scolded by the Pastor? Would he be forced to resign from being a deacon? How would the church family perceive his word when he was asked to teach a class or counsel someone?

Yet, I would point out that in the Bible, there are Biblical accounts of alien craft in Ezekiel Chapter 1 (KJV), as well as II Kings 2:11 (KJV). In my previous book, "The Chariots Flew Then and Still Do today!" I describe the proper translation from the Hebrew using trans interpretation of incident descriptions in what would be a corrected observed assessment.[2]

## Confirmation in Art as Witness

The next big fault of religions that I mentioned in my previous work[3] is the religious paintings that clearly relayed the observance of a UFO in them.[4] They are as follows.

Moses depicted in receiving the Ten Commandments a UFO in the background with flames. It was found on a wood drawer from a piece of furniture and is kept at earls D'Oltremond, in Belgium,

The Baptism of Christ, a disk-shaped object shining beams on John the Baptist and Jesus, was painted in 1710 by the Flemish artist Aert De Gelder and shown in the Fitzwilliam Museum.

Two saucers are seen on either side of Christ. 17th-century fresco of the crucifixion is kept at the Svetishoveli Cathedral in Mtskheta, Georgia.

A Painting by Paolo Uccello in circa 1460-1465 hangs in the Academy of Florence. A UFO is seen near Jesus.

A painting of the Crucifixion in 1350 hangs above the altar at the Visoki Decani Monastery in Kosovo, Yugoslavia.

The painting shows a UFO in the upper left and upper right corners of the painting, with one man in each of the UFOs. When enlarged, the two alien men can be clearly seen.

---

[2] Pleune D.R.E., Ronald, (2019. Line 122-123) *The Chariots Flew Then and Still Do Today.* Conneaut Lake, PA: Page Publishing, Inc.

[3] Ibid. 54

[4] "The UFO Times," 2006-2007. *In Religious Art.* https://www.theufotimes.com/contents/News_11%20.html.

A painting by Bonaventura Salimbeni in 1600 titled "Glorification of the Eucharist" hangs in the church of San Lorenao in San Pietro, Montalcino, Italy. It appears to show Jesus and God holding onto the antennae of a Sputnik Satellite-type of device.

A fresco depicting the Madonna and Christ-child shows a UFO hovering in the background in the back of the Madonna. A close-up picture of the UFO shows details of the UFO, including portholes. Painted by Domenico Ghirlandaio (1449-1494) and hangs as part of the Loeser collection in the Palazzo Vecchio.

A picture of Jesus and Mary above lenticular clouds (which in reality look like a host of UFOs) and is titled "The Miracle of the Snow," painted by Masolina Da Panicale (1383-1440), and hangs at the church of Santa Maria Maggiore, Florence, Italy.

## Divine or Delusion

The time has come that a very sensible question is asked. "Why would religious paintings have UFOs depicted in them if they weren't real?" If the painter was religious and took pride and accuracy to make the paintings, he would have been equally passionate in portraying the UFO in them. Extensive research about De Gelder has not produced a reason for the UFO…but I would offer an explanation here that mirror images the text of II Timothy 3:16 (KJV) by stating that possibly De Gelder painted the truth through "inspiration," that is to say that it was by way of mental telepathy or impulses from an ET entity.

We may ask, "to what extent does "Inspiration" or "Mental Impulses/Telepathy" go? Does it occur today? We know that in the Billy Meier story, one of Billy's first contacts, known as Semjase stated that she would be in contact with him as needed through "thought-transmission.[5] She

---

[5] Billy Meier, "Contact 001, line 70" *They Fly*, January 28, 1975, http://www.theyfly.com/.

does, in fact, affirm that other aliens do indeed communicate only telepathically but in that same sentence states that their knowledge of that in 1975 is limited to "as far as we (Plejaren) know." [6]

There is a further explanation on the subject by another Plejaren teacher of Billy's by the name of Ptaah, which focuses on "unconscious thought impulses." These are brief thoughts that are sent to the human brain and usually to those in various fields of science where a scientist (s) is stuck in figuring out a matter. These thought impulses began in 1844 and are no longer carried out on a large scale but in limited form to prevent negative outcomes such as worse things than what has already happened. [7]

The subject is worthy of further examination since alien contact and influence can indeed come through what the Bible calls "inspiration." During the Apollo 11 moon landing on July 21, 1969, NASA Astronaut Neil Armstrong testified that the "Aliens have a base on the Moon and told us in no uncertain terms to get off and stay off the Moon."[8]

So, if Christianity holds that "inspiration" (mental telepathy) comes from no one else except God, does that mean that God is kicking the U.S. astronauts off the moon? And is there really a God that the Bible claims in charge according to the Bible?

---

[6] Billy Meier, "Contact 002, line 30" *They Fly,* February 3, 1975, http://www.theyfly.com/.

[7] Billy Meier, "Contact 567," *They Fly,* July 6, 2013, http://www.theyfly.com/

[8] UFO Sightings by Astronauts. *Neil Armstrong and Edwin Aldrin.* https://www.syti.net/UFOSightings.html.

# Chapter 2

# Finding the Real Truth

**Reality of Ufology**

Today, there are programs on TV that give proof of alien technology, show alien craft in the air, and most recently, the U.S. Government admitted that there have been actual sightings of UFOs.[9] Bringing this topic to a more personal level, I learned in the summer of 2016 how to signal UFO with a floodlight using a flashing code. Since 2016, my signaling efforts, along with my wife and other witnesses that we invite, have contacted 206 alien craft, which in turn flash their light back at us as an acknowledgment of our "hello," have flown just a few hundred feet over our heads all lit up, hovered a few feet off the ground 300 ft. from us on August 8, 2016, swiftly passed by me within an estimated distance of 200 ft. and gave off a huge light (about 60 ft. in diameter) as well as emitting a wave of cold air, and on another occasion gave off a huge light of about the same diameter within 300 ft. of myself and another witness.

In the spring/early summer of 1974, right after breakfast on a certain cloudless day, I was looking out the kitchen window….and there it was, a UFO hovering about 500 ft. above the back yard. I didn't go looking for it; it just appeared as I was gazing out in the backyard thinking of

---

[9] History, September 19, 2019. *Navy Confirms UFO Videos Are Real and Show Unidentified Arial Phenomena.* History.com/news/navy- confirms-ufo-videos-real.

things I had to do that Saturday. Though I was interested in ufology, and it was the first time I had ever seen a UFO, I did not purposefully seek alien life.

Today, TV programs, news reports, books, and internet videos of UFOs prove that there actually is UFO. In the greater Christian community, the populace scoffs at such documentation. My wife and I take people out late at night, and we show them the UFO as we send a light signal for them, and many times, we get a signal back from them as they move along in space. A few times, they have come close enough that the full outline of the UFO can be seen. No, these are not government ships. Governments of the world do not have the technology that video-recorded alien ships have. Stop and think, if the US or any other country had the technology that ET's have, there would be no need to have several-stage rockets going to the moon…the space ship would easily take off, land on the moon (or Mars, for that matter) and with no effort return to earth in a breakneck speed to make a soft landing at whatever airbase was designated. We must remember that the Plejaren are 3,500 years ahead of earth humans, as recorded by Billy Meier.[10]

In brief, there is no question of the reality of UFOs. But there still is the question of how they fit into Biblical History… that's really the hang-up that the Christian Community struggles with. So, where do they meet, and what has their effect on humankind been? The answer is to follow, and it must be met with a broad and open mind.

The Chronology of Earth History

I would suggest you begin with reading the book "Light Years" by Gary Kinder to get a good understanding of the reality of Plejaren. It is easy to read, not excessively long, yet filled with information that will whet your appetite in wanting to learn more about the Plejaren and the history of mankind on earth.

---

[10] Osborn, Maurice (2009, 39-40) *Plejaren Human Beings.* www.oocities.org/maurice_osborn/E504-2.htm.

*God, The Grandest Illusion*

Next, go to the website *theyfly.com* and begin reading the contact reports in consecutive order. A good overall picture of the "Chronological History of Mankind" was furnished by Christian Frehner (Frehner 2019, email) and can be seen below. The dating of events has been more accurately shown through the corrective action of Billy Meier's administrator Christian Frehner.

- 22 Million B.C. The first Lyrans come to Earth and colonize.
- 387,000 B.C. 144,207 Lyrans come to Earth and settle here, forever changing the genetics of Earthman.
- 228,000 B.C. A Lyran leader named Asael leads 360,000 Lyrans to a new home in the Plejaren.
- 226,000 B.C. Asael dies, and his daughter Plejara becomes the ruler. The system's name was changed to "Plejaren System."
- 225,000 B.C. Plejaran scout ships discover Earth, and colonies are founded here and on Mars and Malona.
- 196,000 B.C. War breaks out on Earth, and people are evacuated to the Plejaren. Forty years Later, Malona destroys itself and becomes the asteroid belt. Mars is thrown out of orbit, and all life is gone.
- 116,000 B.C. For the past 80,000 years, several small colonies have been tried by the Lyrans-mostly exiled criminals.
- 71,344 B.C. The Great Pyramids were built in Egypt, China, and South America by Lyrans.
- 58,000 B.C. The Great Plan. The Plejaren build a great society on Earth that lasts for almost 10,000 years.
- 48,000 B.C. Ishwish Pelegon comes to Earth and builds a wonderful society that lasts for around 10,000 years.
- 31,000 B.C. Atlantis is founded by Atlant, who comes with his people from the Barnard Star system.
- 30,500 B.C. The great city of Mu is founded by Muras, the father of Atlant's wife, Karyatide. His empire is sometimes called Lemuria.
- 30,000 B.C. The black race comes from Sirius.

- 16,000 B.C. Arus is exiled from Earth for trying to start wars. He hides out with his followers in the Beta Centauri star system.
- 13,500 B.C. Arus and his men return to Earth and settle in Hyperborea, which is the current location of Florida.
- 13,000 B.C. The scientist Semjasa, the second in command to Arus, creates two Adams, who bear a child named Seth. This becomes the legend of **Adam and Eve**.
- 11,000 B.C. Arus II attacks the Sumerians, who flee into the mountains.
- 11,000 B.C. A group of ETs of unknown origin arrives, led by a leader named Viracocoha, who controlled the city of Tiahuanaco. His base was on an island named Mot. He provided the inhabitants of Easter Island the tools to build the strange statues that represent him.
- 9498 B.C. Atlantis and Mu destroy each other and ruin the planet. The air is not breathable for 50 years. All survivors are driven underground.
- 9448 B.C. Jehovan, the third son of Arus XI, takes over the three remaining tribes left on Earth and becomes the ruler.
- 8239 B.C. The Destroyer Comet passes closely by Earth and causes the Atlantic Ocean to part.
- **8104 B.C. The Biblical Flood.**
- 6000 B.C. Venus is pulled out of its orbit around the planet Uranus by the Destroyer Comet and orbit around the sun.
- 5981 B.C. The Destroyer Comet comes close to Earth, causing great destruction. It also changes the orbit of Venus.
- 5000 B.C. Jehav, the son of Jehovan, murders his father and takes over rulership.
- 4930 B.C. The Destroyer Comet once again passes close by Earth, causing tidal waves of destruction.
- 1500 B.C. The Destroyer Comet passes by Earth, causing the Santorini Volcano to erupt. It also pulls Venus into its current orbit around the sun.
- 1320 B.C. Jehav is murdered by his son, Arussem, who has two sons named Salem and Ptaah.

- 1010 B.C. Arussem is driven out of power by his sons and hides out under the Great Pyramid with his followers. They call themselves the Bafath.
- 32 A. D. Jmmanuel is crucified on a Y-shaped stake and survives.

Corrections by Christian Frehner on the 1/31/2019.

## The Judeo-Christian History

The above record of the Chronology of the Earth can seem overwhelming, so what is needed is a breakdown of it as laid out in Contact Report #70. It is precise in explaining the alien leadership of mankind and the history of what we know today as the Hebrews. It is important to understand who the Hebraon/ Hebrons/Hebrew were as described in the 70th Contact Report by Semjase, one of Billy Meier's instructors.[11]

It is suggested that though the following information is a good "under the microscope" view of what we know as the Hebrew people, there is more detail regarding the worship of "God" from the Garden of Eden through the birth of Abraham in Sumeria and his journey to Judea, including his parents and grandparents being involved in the carving and worship of idols, and going back in time as to who on Abraham's genealogical list did or did not worship God which is recorded in my book "The Chariots Flew Then and Still Do Today!" The book is available through Amazon, Amazon Kindle, Barnes & Noble, and Google Play & iTunes.

Line 140; "The third Earth people was actually, in and of itself, no such thing, because it concerned a very widely disseminated alliance of gypsies, which was interspersed with Jehavon\'s spies and saboteurs, who, in unity with the gypsies, brought about dissension everywhere, greedily drawing everything to themselves and were always constantly

---

[11] Billy Meier, "Contact 70, line 140" *They Fly*, January 6, 1977, http://www.theyfly.com/.

eager to murder, burn and rob, for which reason one named them the Hebrons by the original language of our forefathers, therefore Hebraon and later then Hebrons."

The following is a simplistic breakdown of those that led the Hebrews as provided and corrected by the head administrator, Christian Frehner, for Billy Meier.[12]

**First** group of earth people- descendants of Armus from the region of Armenia

**Second** group of earth people- very distant descendants of the Aryans (of Arus II)

**Third** group of earth people- Hebrew (name development from Hebraon to Hebrons to Hebrew)

Arus I- Contact #70, Line 125- **133,000** yrs. ago

Contact #70, Line 129- Conquered land in northern regions where the climate was good (before the Noahic Flood)

Contact #70, Line 132- Constantly troubled Atlantis& Mu until finally destroyed centuries later (*which would come in 9498 BC per the Chronology of Earth*)

Arus II- Contact #70, Line 131, Came from the north, conquered India, Pakistan, and Persia, etc. (*the approx. date would be before or after his attack on the Sumerians in 11,000 BC*)

Arus XI- Contact #70, Line 136- **4023 BC**, Distant descendent of Arus I; Murdered by 3rd born son Jehavon.

---

[12] Billy Meier, "Contact 70, line 110-181," *They Fly,* January 6, 1977, http://www.theyfly.com/.

*God, The Grandest Illusion*

Jehavon- Contact #70, Line 145- **3683 BC** (Corrected date); Murdered by his only son **Jehav** who had three sons, Line 136; and took overruling "hater people" (Hebrews), three other groups, and the Hyperboreans.

Jehav- Contact Report #70, Line 146- **3343 BC** (Corrected date); was a wicked ruler and had three sons: Arussem, Ptaah, and Salam.

1st son Arussem was addicted to power and murdered his father Jehav.

Ptah and Salam worked together and expelled Arussem and 72,000 followers, Contact Report #70, line 151.

Contact Report #70, Line 153- After (Arussem) was expelled by Ptaah and Salam, he returned to Earth and established a base below the Pyramids known as the Giza Intelligences.

Contact Report #70, Line 158- **1010 BC**, Arussem ruled "Giza Intelligences" under the Great Pyramid.

Henn (called Jehovah)- Line 158- in **3010 BC** ousted Arussem.

Kamagol I -Contact Report #70, Line 159-160- **2080 BC;** ousted his nephew Henn/Jehovah and **forced all earthly religions under his control, created vicious cults and confusion,** and **demanded human blood,** which is partially practiced until this day. Line 162, overthrown by Kamagol II; Kamagol I imprisoned and died in a dungeon.

Kamagol II- Contact Report #70, line 162, overthrew Kamagol I and "performed monstrous mass murdering of earth-born terrestrial human beings, which he slapped under his religious power through many kinds of means. He departed this world on December 27, 1976.

Ptaah& Salam- led further rule by common agreement, Contact Report #70, Line 168.

Ptaah dies after 93 years of his ruling time, Contact Report #70, Line 170.

Salam continued his ruling until 2,040 terrestrial years ago.

Plejos- Contact Report #70, Line 170- Son of Salam, was handed over the command 2,040 years ago (from the year 1977) = 63 BC; placed himself and his people under the home form of government, namely that of spiritual leaders. Line 171, positioned he and his people under the guidance of the "High Council." Contact Report #70, Line 172- 1,994 years ago (from 1977) which equals 17 BC, Plejos returned to the home-worlds.

To sum it up, all these personages are IHWH/JHWH, pronounced "Ischwisch" which is to say a King of Wisdom, or simply "God," and eventually passes away while another IHWH/JHWH (God) takes over. **Henn, who was labeled the 'Unjust Cruel one" and called himself "Jehovah,"** passed away 2,150 years prior to the 39th contact which was on December 3, 1975. His passing would have been in 175 BC.

This is the last JHWH/IHWH (King of Wisdom or "God") of the Hebrew as well as the Christian and Muslim faiths, which are defined in the next section. Thus, there is no God that is the Creator of life.

## Identifying God

The above information sounds overwhelming, but it does give the reader some insight into the history of the Hebrew people and who was considered "God." To understand the Biblical confusion of the personage of God, we turn to what the Plejaren revealed to Billy Meier, which is quoted from contact reports Billy had with various teachers and the development of the Goblet of the Truth. There are more quotes from the contact reports and the Goblet of the Truth, but the following quotes are sufficient to drive home the fact that the belief in a God is just a fabulation and delusion.

From Semjase: Contact #1
Line 47; A god is only a governor as well as a human being who powerfully or dictatorially reigns over his fellowmen. Line 48; God is not Creation but only one of its creatures, like all creatures who are dependent upon Creation. [13]

From Semjase: Contact #3
Line 27; In their limited reasoning, Earth humans would venerate us as gods just as they did in former times; on the other hand, many people among them—criminal and power-hungry people—would gain possession of our beam ships.[14]

From Semjase: Contact #5
The leaders were very developed and portrayed themselves to be Gods of man. They were called Kings of Wisdom, by the word IHWH, which on Earth means GOD.[15]

From Semjase: Contact #5
Line 182; on the home planet dissension broke out again because once again, the scientists set themselves up as gods and struck the peoples into bondage.[16]

From Semjase: Contact #11
Line 157; If the Earth human being now finally recognizes and acknowledges this truth, completely frees himself from all religions, sects, and other erroneous teachings and their delusional imaginations,

---

[13] Billy Meier, "Contact 001, line 47-48," *They Fly*, January 28, 1975, http://www.theyfly.com/.

[14] Billy Meier, "Contact 003, line 27-30," *They Fly*, February 8, 1975, http://www.theyfly.com/.

[15] Billy Meier, "Contact 005, line 153," *They Fly*, February 16, 1975, http://www.theyfly.com/.

[16] Ibid, line 182.

and finally aligns himself with the spiritual and creational laws, then he has triumphed.[17]

From Semjase: Contact #18
Line 100; The constant repetition of this false religious teaching causes the believers to find imagined and deceitful fulfillment and subject themselves to an evil delusion that prevents all their rationality pertaining to consciousness, whereby their spiritual-intellectual thoughts are hindered and oppressed and enslaved.[18]

From Ptaah: (Semjase's father): Contact #32
Line 315; If Semjase has only spoken in a negative form about the Earth religions so far, this finds its justification in that by this, the terrestrial mankind had to be made aware of the falseness and unreality of their religions, because these are in every form evil and unreal, like it is not the case in these forms, in any of the worlds known to us from anywhere else in the Universe.[19]

From Ptaah: (Semjase's father): Contact #32
Line 344-346; The Creation, however, is the vastest, the mightiest, and the glory itself.

Through various circumstances, and not least through the megalomania of the human creatures, were JHWH/IHWHs, kings of wisdom, leaders of the people, and leaders of the human race, **which according to Earth human terms were known as GOD, pressed into the term-related form of a Creator, and deceitfully declared as the highest in the Universe, namely the Creation itself.** This is still evident today

---

[17] Billy Meier, "Contact 11, line 157-158," *They Fly*, April 15, 1975, http://www.theyfly.com/.

[18] Billy Meier, "Contact 18, line 100," *They Fly*, May 15, 1975, http://www.theyfly.com/.

[19] Billy Meier, "Contact 32, line 315," *They Fly*, September 8, 1975, http://www.theyfly.com/.

on the addressing form of the Earth humans when they refer to their GOD as the CREATOR.[20]

Not only do the contact reports of Billy Meier's conversations with highly intelligent humans from Erra state that there is no such thing as a God, but so does the Goblet of the Truth, as indicated below from various verses below.

Goblet of the Truth

Believers in a god or tin gods say that their god or tin god may bestow good on them in this world and good in the future world, and they beg with blind submissiveness that their god or tin god may save them from the anguish of the fire of the shadow world (hell) and its princes; however neither a god nor a tin god is truthfully given, because they are only imaginary forms which are fabulated (invented) by yourselves without responsibility and which have no might even to make a single hair on your head turn grey; and therefore the shadow world (hell) and its fire and the prince of the shadow world (prince of hell) are only inventions by irresponsible and humorless ones amongst you who have fallen victim to a delusion of belief, as well as their own might which they wish to wield over you in order to obtain great gain of all kinds from it; and therefore the shadow world (hell) is no place, because truly it is a state in your head (consciousness) and a mentality (thoughts, feelings and psyche).

If you obey your god or tin gods in your belief, then you will receive your share according to your belief, and its merit then consider that it is not a god or a tin god which effectuates the things that you believe, but only the might of your thoughts and your inner world (consciousness).[21]

---

[20] Billy Meier, "Contact 32, line 344-346," *They Fly*, September 8, 1975, http://www.theyfly.com/.

[21] Billy Meier, *Goblet of the Truth*, (Canada:-Landsgruppe Canada, 2015, 53).

*Dr. Ron Pleune*

Goblet of the Truth [22]

And consider, there is neither a god nor tin gods nor people of your kind (human beings) and demons or either liberators (angels) and venerable ones (holy ones) who can reanimate a dead person (deceased person) because when someone dies the spirit escapes into the realm of invisibility (other world) and cannot return to the deceased body because this is irreversibly connected to death.[23]

Goblet of the Truth

Do not wait for your gods and tin gods to come to you in the shadow of clouds and with liberators (angels) to judge you and decide in equitableness (fairness) whether you will go into the fire of the shadow world (hell) or into heaven in their paradise (realm of gods and tin gods); truly, this will not happen, because you will not return to your gods or your tin gods because they are inventions of your own without any power and any existence and reality, but are only imagined unsubstantial delusions.

As a person of your kind (human being), your dwelling is the world on which you live, and as such, you can only raise yourselves into the firmament (space/universe) with flying craft that you build for yourselves, in order for you to be able to cross the air of Earth and the firmaments (space/universe); but even with such flying craft you cannot reach the heaven of one of your invented gods or tin gods (realm of gods and tin gods), because the heaven and its gods and tin gods (realm of gods and tin gods) are really only inventions of your imaginations.

In you, lives the spirit, which is a minute part of the formation (Creation), therefore you are also a part of the formation (Creation); however, your body is of your world, and when you die then it will cease to be and will not return, just as it will not cross over into a heaven of your gods and tin

---

[22] Ibid. 67.

[23] Ibid. 55.

gods and not into a paradise (the realm of gods and tin gods), but will cease to be; only your form of the spirit in you is subject to reincarnation and intended to one day return to the formation (Creation) in order to become one with it, although you as a person cease to exist and will no longer continue to be such.[24]

Goblet of the Truth

And know that the laws and recommendations of the primal raising (Creation) establish (confirm) that there is no primal raising (Creation) except for it; therefore, there are neither gods nor tin gods, nor people of your kind (human beings) or liberators (angels) and demons who stand above it; and so know that those who possess the true knowledge about the real truth are the keepers of equitableness (fairness) whom you shall follow so that you too will be fair and connected to equitableness (fairness).[25]

## Creation

Having identified what the term or personage of "God" is as nothing more than extraterrestrial beings that had superior knowledge and wisdom to bring together terrestrial mankind for the purpose of exploitation and servitude to them, the next endeavor is to define what Creation is and how it, not God, brought mankind into existence.

This particular subject divides the religious communities into basically two camps, the "young world" conviction, and the "old world" conviction.

For years Christians have been taught that the Bible describes the Truth about creation, yet this statement is full of holes… it just doesn't hold water! Look at the different scholars that worked on the dating of

---

[24] Ibid. 77.

[25] Wikipedia, s.v. "Biblical Literalist Chronology," last modified July 13, 2018, https://en.wikipedia.org/wiki/Biblical_literalist_chronology.

Biblical Creation such as "Archbishop James Ussher, who placed it in 4,004 BCE, Isaac Newton in 4,000 BCE, Martin Luther in 3,961 BCE, the traditional Jewish date of 3,760 BCE, and the traditional Greek Orthodox date, based on the Septuagint, of 5,009 BCE. " [26]

The dating of Biblical history is also complicated by the fact that names of consecutive genealogical listings are not reliable. Some texts skip generations because a son was not prominent or was not the first-born of the family. The individual could also be a grandson from many later generations! To confound matters even greater, there are no dates of when a person was born or died…only events in the history of a group, region, city, kingship, war or other notable event.[27]

Thus, incorrect "best estimates would be 8,000 to 10,000 BC for the time of the flood and 12,000 to 13,000 BC for the time of Adam."[28] Consider that The King James Bible lists a genealogy going back to Adam as being about 4,000 years B.C., yet the Septuagint approximately 12,000 years BC.[29]

The conclusion is that these dates are severely corrupt because, once again they are made by man's guesswork. The authoritative word is not from historians or scientists who use various instruments and techniques to date something; they can only give us a hazy picture at best of creation and the history behind it. Historians and Scientists are blinded by the fact that what they discover has to be from "their own deductions rather than considering that there are human entities who know all about our world and universe…all they have to do is contact Billy Meier and ask the questions or review the information on the

---

[26] "Biblical Old Testament Chronology," accessed October 26, 2018, http://www.accuracyingenesis.com/chronology.htm.

[27] Ibid.

[28] Ibid.

[29] David R. Montgomery, *The Rocks Don't Lie* (New York: W. W. Norton and Company, 2012), 170-178.

website *theyfly.com*. Let's think about the rationality and logic in this. If you pick up the Bible and read the weird things that are unexplainable (other than using the excuse that "God did it"), people would think that the Bible is a bunch of non-believable happenings.

The historians use the excuse "we can prove that Sodom and Gomorrah existed, but we can't prove the destruction of it other than "what the Bible says." And because of that very statement people accept it as truth. Scientists are more skeptical because they want the credit for "proving" or "finding" something. They don't want to rely on alien technology or alien records that are actually written down and proven to be factual. Yet I challenge them to search the authentic and proven evidence of the pictures of the Plejaren ships taken by Billy Meier, various artifacts and the authenticated fulfilled prophecies and predictions that are on the *theyfly.com* website and the contact reports that give scientific data that NASA didn't even know but was later proven to be 100% true.

The Bible states the account of Noah's flood, yet archeology points out there were many floods, and each had its own extent of flooding the earth. This can be seen in the various layers of earth, formations, and the testing of rocks, fossils, and artifacts.

David R. Montgomery, Geologist, and author of *The Rocks Don't Lie*, investigates Noah's Flood and finds that there are many flood stories that were regional in nature, not universal (worldwide), such as the Babylonian account, the Sumerian account, the Pacific Islands account, Chinese account, Mesopotamian and the Klamath Indian story in Oregon.[30]

The case for a worldwide flood was dismantled as the 20th Century lumbered along during debates amongst creationists and theologians. I remember the debates between us high school students very well, some impromptu in the halls and some in the History class. Presently, as a non-Christian, I look back fifty years as a teenager and former fundamental evangelical Christian, and think of how I dogmatically

---

[30] Ibid.

held the Bible as being without error, yet in the back of my mind, I was saying to myself, "there's something more to the story…things just don't seem to be adding up."

The capstone issue was the alternative explanation for the Siberian Mammoth carcasses. Eventually, religious creationists and geological proponents clashed in which "…radically conservative Christians broke with those who acknowledged scientific findings and began to **ignore, selectively cherry-pick, and actively undermine** science to support their favorite literal interpretation of the Bible. Today we know them as creationists."[31]

The battle continues as aptly described in the *Washington Post* in 2016 when an article was published regarding the young world theory and the old world theory of when dinosaurs existed, whether they rode out Noah's flood or not, and when the dinosaurs went extinct.[32] A creationist known as Ken Ham sides with the "young world" theory that the planet is approximately 6,000 years old, as advertised at the "Ark Encounter" theme park in Williamston, KY.

However, there is a very large hole in Ken Ham's stand on how old the Earth is. Bodie Hodge, a proponent of the same stand, who wrote *Dinosaurs, Dating, and the Age of the Earth*.[33]

---

[31] Vicky Hallett, "Now There's a Theory that Noah Saved Dinosaurs from the Flood," *Washington Post*, December 30, 2016, https://www.washingtonpost.com/national/health-science/now- theres-a-theory-that-dinosaurs-were-wiped-out-in-noahs-flood/2016/12/30/92bec544-cc59-11e6-a747-d03044780a02_story.html?noredirect=on&utm_term=.58d2232dbed4

[32] Bodie Hodge, "Dinosaurs, Dating, and the Age of the Earth," January 2, 2006, https://answersingenesis.org/dinosaurs/when-did-dinosaurs- live/dinosaurs-dating-and-the-age-of-the-earth/.

[33] "Why Disagreement on Dating the Old Testament Chronology," *Genesis Research*, accessed October 29, 2018, http://www.accuracyingenesis.com/.

So, what are the points of truth that need to be held?

1. The genealogies in the Bible do not add up to about 6,000 years. If he looks at, with an open mind, the "Usher Method" of chronological calculations using the Masoretic listings of genealogies, the birth date of BC is stated as 4,004. If the Septuagint listing is used, the date is 5,490. Yet if the "Patriarchal-Age Method is used, the Masoretic listing takes the date of BC to 10,842, and the Septuagint to 12,028. Noting the arguments of each "Method," there is no known answer to the dating of the earth or creation.[34]

2. Carbon 14, the most commonly used isotope for dating plants and animals, is limited in its accuracy to items less than 60,000 years old.[35] You will find people on both sides of the fence when it comes to dating rocks, bones, and wood. The point to remember is the question of what can be used to date certain items cannot date other items.

   Gregory Weber addresses the issue in "Answers to Creationist Attacks on Carbon-14 Dating" when he points out that "radiocarbon (c_14) dating is one of the most reliable of all the radiometric dating methods."[36]

3. Yet, on the other hand, radiometric dating is very accurate in dating specific geologic events. In fact, radiometric dating is a very accurate way to date the Earth.[37] Looking at modern radiometric dating, techniques have been tested and fine-tuned continually since the 1960's and have resulted in approximately forty different dating techniques, and when applied to samples,

---

[34] Gregory Weber, "Answers to Creationist Attacks on Carbon 14 Dating," *Christian/Evolution Journal 3*, no. 2 (Spring 1982): 23-29.

[35] Ibid.

[36] "Q and A on Radiometric Dating," *UCSB ScienceLine*, April 3, 2012, http://scienceline.ucsb.edu/getkey.php?key=2901.

[37] Wikipedia, s.v. "Age of the Earth," last modified October 29, 2018.

these varying techniques are in "very close agreement on the age of the material."[38]

A more comprehensive and in-depth look at Creation instead of God is the multifaceted description that Billy Meier had given in 1993. It gives one the true essence of Creation as not only planets and stars and that which we see but of the all-embracing make-up of who we are as presented below.[39]

1. The Creation is the immeasurable mystery suspended in the immeasurable expanse.
2. The Creation is identical to 'Universal Consciousness', which guides and prevails in the BEING of consciousness; it is a double-helix, egg-shaped configuration that simultaneously constitutes the Universe in its growing expansion. Its pulsating double-helix arms live as a spiritual energy, while rotating against each other.
3. The Universe is the Creation's internal and external body.
4. The Creation— through its entirety pulsate the Universal 'Gemut' (a non-translatable German term for the spiritual counterpart to the psyche) and the Universal Consciousness, the power of life and existence in general.
5. The Creation pervades everything, and everything pervades the Creation, therefore forming oneness within itself. Within this oneness occur all life and all of the evolution allotted to it.
6. The Creation has the identical developmental and evolutionary process as every life form,— however, its values of time are anchored in very high values indeed.

---

[38] Meier, Billy (1993 Document) "What is the Creation?" https://ca.figu.org/what-is-the-creation-.html.

[39] Billy Meier, "Contact 008, line 1-13," *They Fly*, March 18, 1975, http://www.theyfly.com/.

7. The Creation itself exists in a conscious creative state for seven Great-Times.— Subsequently, it lays dormant for an equal number of Great-Times, but this time they last seven times as long. Following this period, the Creation is awake to create once again for a period seven times as longer once again than the previous one. (One Great-Time is equal to 311,040,000,000,000 terrestrial years; seven Great-Times add up to 2,177,280,000,000,000 terrestrial years, also called an eternity; 7 x 7 Great-Times make one All-GreatTime.)

8. The Creation is the Creation, and there exists no Creation other than it within its own Universe. The Creation is the Creation of all creations such as the Universe, the galaxies, stars, earths (earth is equivalent to 'planets' in this context), skies, light and darkness, time, space, and all multitudes of life forms in existence, each according to its own species.

9. The Creation is justice, love, strength, wisdom, knowledge, compassion, freedom, mercy, laws, directive, alliance, fulfillment, evolution, life, support, joy, beauty, peace, infallibility, equilibrium, spirit, forever, logic, growth, perfection, contentment, inexhaustibility, omnipotence, sweetness, infinity, solidarity, perception, harkening, elevation, the Sohar, gentleness, lucidity, purity, transformation, origin, future, power, reverence, allness, and BEING.

10. The Creation is the BEING and non-BEING of life. It is the most immense mass of spiritual energy in the Universe.

11. The Creation is spirit in its purest form and immeasurable in its wisdom, knowledge, love, and harmony in truth.

12. The Creation is a spiritually dynamic, pure-spirit energy that prevails over everything. Incomprehensible for human beings, it is active, creative wisdom in the midst of its own incessant evolution; it is all-encompassing for all times.

13. The Creation is verity, the all-embracing, solace, comprehensiveness, guidance, equality, accuracy, cognition,

empirical knowledge, admonition, discipline, recollection, revelation, praise, perfection, explanation, and direction.

14. The Creation is the path of life; it is nature, light, fire, and contemplation; The Creation is consciousness, and it is omnipresent.

From the points above, we gain the understanding that Creation is not just something to look at, but an actual partpiece of every individual to identify with, come to know in a fuller measure, a power that has sustained mankind and yet expresses its naturalness in the composition of chemical processes that even act adversely to mankind in which life is brought to face death gradually or suddenly.

Creation is not only what we physically feel, such as with flesh and bone, but it is also intricately woven into our psyche as to our thoughts, prejudices, likes, dislikes, and a myriad of emotions and senses that help us in the appreciation of nature, people, seasons, the functions of the sun, moon, stars and the ongoing of laws of the universe that we are not even cognizant of yet.

In Contact Report #8, Billy Meier meets with his main teacher from the Pleiades by the name of Semjase. One of the questions that he has involves "matter" and how it is formed by Creation...not by a God!!! To understand this, you need to grasp the fact that Creation is Spirit in its purest form. There is nothing higher than Creation.

Semjase states that matter is a tangible idea;[40] it is a solid form of energy that is tangible. It is also highly focused and highly concentrated which in turn can be changed into solid matter. This will result in the creation of the basic building blocks of solid matter; neutron, proton and electron. These come to form the atoms and the large number of the chemical compounds which in their three different states of matter form the solid outer shell which is known by earth scientists. Solid

---

40 Ibid. lines17-25.

matter as well as primal energy is equivalent in all respect. Therefore, primal energy is fundamental matter and primal matter is absolute energy. The conclusion is that absolutely everything in the universe is made of matter or energy. Yet, the two concepts of energy and matter are fundamentally one and the same consisting of two different forms known as coarse- substantial and the other as fine fluidal. More simply, coarse-substantial equates to matter, and fine fluidal as energy.

Semjase explains to Billy Meier that matter is the embodiment of an idea.[41] Energy is fine-fluidal matter and a mass is just highly concentrated and condensed. Both of these can be reproduced with an apparatus that mankind has pursued in different forms. Under normal conditions, they are created naturally, specifically by spiritual force which precedes the idea. Thus, Creation is fundamentally responsible; an immense spiritual form; a factor which in turn embodies primal energy and results in "the idea." This "idea," through the force of the spirit (which in turn embodies energy) compresses and concentrates the idea than to a fine-fluidal energy which is then condensed through a still higher concentration into coarse-substantial that is to say, "matter". Semjase affirms to Billy that the whole universe is just an idea concentrated and compressed into the fine-fluidal and coarse-substantial energy.[42]

So, let's look at a simpler way of describing the process. We might say this: The Spirit of Creation that has immense power and can take an idea (fine fluidal state), and can compress it with all the laws of science...then compress it even harder to create something tangible, that is to say, coarse substantial state.

---

41  Ibid. lines 24-25.

42  Billy Meier, "Contact 70, line 110-181," *They Fly,* January 6, 1977, http://www.theyfly.com/.

*Dr. Ron Pleune*

# The struggle of Our Ancestry

This topic is truly unique because for the Christian the subject of God has always existed and revealed in various texts, parchments, versions, etc. But there is the untold story of how God came to be and has influenced us to this very day. Christians (protestant and independent from a multitude of definitions), Muslims, Mormons, Catholics, and untold denominations as well as splinter-groups refuse to move out of their comfort zone to discover the real truth of how they came to believe their sacred writings.

For most people, the information will be hard to swallow. The question here is, why is this case? The answers are varied, and here is some of what holds people in ignorance.

1) People feel comfortable in what they know.
2) People do not want to explore what is yet to be known.
3) The leadership advises them that there is nothing to add to the history of their faith from what the Bible has recorded.
4) The leadership refuses to amend religious history because it will make the leadership look stupid and make what has been taught a weak link in their teaching and faith.

There are key statements made by various Plejaren attesting to the events 133,000 years ago as recorded in Contact Report #70,[43] and recorded in the Goblet of the Truth where we need to examine the larger picture of alien influence on mankind as to:

1) Who has influenced our heritage?
2) Why we do not remember our heritage?
3) Why is it that we think and act as we do today?

---

[43] Billy Meier, "Contact 251, pg. 4-25," *They Fly*, February 3, 1995. http://www.theyfly.com/.

*God, The Grandest Illusion*

We have looked at a section of history as indicated in Contact Report #70 concerning the Hebrews, but now we need to expand it much more too all mankind because everyone was influenced prior to 133,000 years ago as Contact Report #251 has recorded. Why? It lays the groundwork for understanding the three questions above regarding Religion, particularly the Christian religion and related religious groups.

Since Contact Report #251 is so long, it will be summarized. The contact report is available for your review by going to theyfly.com, choosing "Billy's Contacts" in the tool bar, then dropping down the page and choosing "List of Pleiadean/Plejaren Contact Reports." A color key is listed for each Contact Report designating whether the entire contact is translated, partial translation, preliminary translation, or not translated yet.

The portion of which is of concern regarding Earth's religious heritage begins after a couple of pages of conversation between Billy Meier and Semjase's father, Ptaah. Specific points are recorded below for the purpose of cutting through an immense amount of detail within approximately 36 pages.[44]

Down through nearly 12 billion years, mankind has had periods of war and peace in outer space. Groups of people emigrated to other galaxies and lost their true ancestry whereby their chroniclers, historians, and others created a different legend about their heritage which resulted in some settling in the Pleiades and others in the region of the Sirius constellation.

Some bred new human races and manipulated their genes. The new life forms turned barbaric in nature, degenerate and cruel with a life span of only 100 years. Two large, genetically-manipulated people fled from the Sirius regions eventually landing in the Lyra regions. Later some settled in China, Japan, and other locations and formed new races. Other genetically manipulated people had been banished to various terrestrial locations, and some found refuge on Mars and Malona/

---

[44] Billy Meier, "Contact 008, line 66, *They Fly*, March 18, 1975. http://www.theyfly.com/.

*Dr. Ron Pleune*

Phaeton until Mars became uninhabitable through cosmic influences and drove them to settle on Earth. Malona/Phaeton eventually was destroyed by fratricidal wars.

The conspirators, (benefactors) who helped the genetically manipulated terrestrial people came to the Earth, became powerful and in time destroyed the Earth peoples' ancestral records. These benefactors elevated themselves to "gods" whereby the population became vassals and believers.

In time, the benefactors (the gods) of the genetically- manipulated people withdrew from Earth but vowing to return. After some time, they (the gods) returned, causing havoc. Some of the benefactors remained benevolent to Earth terrestrials and hoped to one day return to Earth.

It is interesting to note in Contact Report #251 that the genetic manipulation was for the purpose of developing people for various forms of fighting capabilities. The downside was that they would die prematurely which prevented the genetically-manipulated individuals from banding together and rising up against the "over-lords." Genetically manipulated people remained overly entangled in the effect the genes had caused which resulted in fighting, viciousness, barbarism, bloodthirstiness, greed, addiction, emotional malfunctions, and inhumanities…to name a few. **Excuse me; this is exactly what is going on in our society and world today!!!! You can't deny it!!!**

These above results, from genetic manipulation, have been passed down over millions of years and become known as "original sin" in the tale of Adam, Eve, and the devil-like snake in the Garden of Eden. **This single gene has become responsible for the fighting and evil** since time immemorial. Contact Report #251 states that the gene can be rectified if Earth's scientists identify it and reverse it.

In summary, the effects of the genetic manipulation as recorded in Contact Report #251 is as follows.

1) Physical changes to increase fighting capabilities
2) Shortened life span
3) An attitude of viciousness barbarism
4) Thirst for blood
5) Greed
6) Addiction to power
7) Emotional malfunctions
8) Inhumanities
9) Lack of historical knowledge
10) Revenge/retaliation

The flipside of the coin is that if the gene is corrected, mankind will lose his capability to fight, which is really essential for his existence.

Though the gene manipulation altered physical traits which resulted in resistance to environmental influences, there still was a certain amount of barbarity. The gene that was not affected during the gene-manipulation of humans was the one that is responsible for cognizance, comprehension and compliance with the Creation-natural laws…. that is to say all that is balanced and good.

In Contact Report #8, Billy Meier has a conversation with his main teacher, Semjase, and he asks her about a gene that forms the hereditary factor, and she responds, "it is the carrier of hereditary characteristics in the chromosomes." She continues to point out that the age limit is somewhat controlled by chromosomes and is gene conditioned. She points out that "the genes control the cellular functions via the brain and the spirit, and they steer life, regeneration, and decay of the cells. The Chromosomes determine species, shape and gender of the life form... however, "genes over time are also able to change because like everything in the universe, they are also subject to an evolutionary or degenerative process."[45]

The bottom line is that the gene manipulation did not totally dehumanize mankind over the past millions of years, viciousness remains a factor and the battle between good and evil which was identified as "original sin" because humans are not able to find the appropriate paths and ended up clinging to false ideals that frequently originated from religious-sectarian idiocy.

So, when will full contact and disclosure by extraterrestrials occur whereby more and more people will be confronted with the truth that the ET in the past millions of years are the Gods of what were considered myths and fakery?

Contact Report #251 states that at this time ET contacts will occur only with "individuals or certain very small groups including those of a secret military and governmental nature. Mankind will still have those that believe in various false Biblical stories concerning their origin instead of shedding the film of delusional teaching over their eyes and coming to the reality that human beings did not originate on this planet.

## Talmud of Jmmanuel

The question now is, "what credible source should be used for learning about the "Truth" of earth history and Spiritual growth? They are described as follows.

The Contact Reports- These reports are detailed conversations between Billy Meier and those of the DAL and DERN universes (our present universe is the DERN universe), whether in person or telepathically. These revelations were written by Billy Meier, the last of seven prophets.

---

[45] Billy Meier, "Contact 213, Part 1, *They Fly*, December 2, 1986, http://www.theyfly.com/.

Their authenticity is found in 1) personal (one-to- one) contacts as well as telepathic messaging, 2) the information that Billy receives about scientific information is not only provable but tested to be authentic, 3) the prophecies that Billy announces have proven true and complete. The fulfillment of future prophecies is to be seen but relied upon to be fulfilled based on past fulfillment of prophecies that are proven by their actual existence physically and scientifically.

The Goblet of the Truth- The writing of the Laws (of science) and Recommendations for daily living for the fulfillment of life that can be lived through peace, freedom, love, and harmony.

The Talmud of Jmmanuel- The Talmud of Jmmanuel is the writing of Judas Ischkerioth, not Judas Iscariot of the life of Jmmanuel.

The special writings of Billy Meier- Articles written by Billy Meier that announce, explain, warn, give advice, etc., through the wisdom of Billy Meier, the last of seven prophets.

All of the above sources are important, but what is to be focused on now is the Talmud of Jmmanuel.

The Talmud of Jmmanuel was found in 1963 by a Greek Catholic Priest by the name of Isa Rashid and Billy Meier. After they removed the rubble that was obscuring the entryway to a cave, they crawled inside and recovered a composite of ancient scrolls that were wrapped in animal skin that was encased in a dry crumbly resin. Upon close examination, they found that the Aramaic pages were legible and told of the life of a man named Jmmanuel. This man, who was incorrectly identified in the Gospel of Matthew as being named Jesus, told of his life, educating people about the nature of the universe, aspects of life on Earth, the immortality of the human spirit through reincarnation and the way life that is not only liberating but free from illogical constraints, human greed, lust for power and belief-related-delusions.[46]

---

[46] Billy Meier, (2016, LX-LXIV), *Talmud of Jmmanuel*, Landesgruppe, Canada.

By sometime in 1970, the translation of the Talmud of Jmmanuel up through the 36th chapter had been completed and sent to Billy Meier. In 1976, Isa Rashid and his family fled from Jerusalem to Lebanon, where Israeli authorities discovered him. The camp was bombed which forced Isa and his family to move to Baghdad and leave the remaining rolls behind. The fate of the remaining rolls is unknown, possibly burned or stolen and in the hands of someone else. In 1976 Billy Meier learned that Isa Rashid and his family were assassinated in Baghdad.[47]

The tomb cave of Jmmanuel was eventually destroyed by a Plejaren of the name of Quetzal so that the site would not become a place of Christian attraction or worship.[48]

The author of the Talmud of Jmmanuel is Judas Ischkerioth which is not to be confused with Judas Ishariot, Jmmanuel's traitor, and the son of the Pharisee Simeon Ishariot who was from a small settlement called 'Ariot' in Galilee.[49]

This newly found Scripture covers the life of Jmmanuel from birth through the staking of Jmmanuel on a "Y" configuration instead of the false reference of vertical and horizontal cross pieces. The Talmud of Jmmanuel has commentaries throughout the record that explain various situations and circumstances that are named in the Christian make-up of what is called the Gospel of Matthew but also explain additional information about Jmmanuel such as his journey to India, marriage, and having numerous children. The Talmud of Jmmanuel tells us that Jmmanuel eventually arrived in Srinagar, India, where he continued to spread the "teaching of the prophets," and at the age of 111, he died and was buried. Jmmanuel's firstborn son eventually returned to Jerusalem

---

[47] Billy Meier, (2016 XCIV), *Talmud of Jmmanuel*, Landesgruppe, Canada.

[48] Ibid, XXII-XXVI.

[49] Ibid, 562.

and buried his father's teachings that Judas Ischkerioth penned in the cave until their discovery in 1963.[50]

What about the remaining Gospels of Mark and Luke?

The Talmud of Jmmanuel reveals that the Gospel of Luke was written by a literate woman named Fatima of Damascus. The actual person known as Luke, was born approximately 65 years after Jmmanuel in the country of Syria and died at the age of 84 in Greece. Luke was not schooled in reading and writing but he did hear what was written in Matthew and handed it down to be written by the woman Fatima of Damascus. The result of course was that many things were changed, as commonly happens, when given from one person to another.[51]

According to the Plejaren records, the Gospel of Mark was not written by Mark. It was actually through the pen of a scribe who had converted to Christianity early on. The

Gospel was dictated to him by John Mark in June of 69 AD.[52]

So, the authenticity of the Talmud of Jmmanuel rests on solid findings and should be relied upon as being authoritative. The following points are made.

1. They were physically found (1963 in Jerusalem).
2. They were found by two men (Billy and Isa Rashid).
3. They were translated from Aramaic to German. (Originals burned or stolen)

---

[50] Ibid. CXXIV.

[51] Ibid.

[52] Wikipedia s.v. (2019, Document), *List of the Dead Sea Scrolls*, accessed 1/11/2020, https://en.wikipedia.org > wiki > List_of_the_Dead_Sea_Scrolls.

Now, if we were to compare the finding of the Talmud of Jmmanuel to the finding of the Dead Sea Scrolls, one of the major discrepancies of the Dead Sea Scrolls is that the Book of Esther is nonexistent. Yet, if you go to the Bible, Esther is one of the books within it. The question here is this: Should the Bible be thrown out due to the nonexistence of Esther? There are many more discrepancies in the Dead Sea Scrolls as recorded in the "List of the Dead Sea Scrolls."[53]

My point is this, the Talmud of Jmmanuel was written during the time of Jmmanuel which is the first century AD.

They were written in Old Aramaic as was the case in some of the writings of the Dead Sea Scrolls.[54]

The Dead Sea Scrolls were written roughly between 150 BC and 70 AD. The Dead Sea Scrolls were written mostly in Hebrew, some in Aramaic, Greek, Arabic, and Latin.[55]

The difference in parts of the content of the Talmud of Jmmanuel compared to the Dead Sea Scrolls, or for that matter, any other so-called Judeo/Christian writing, is in the fact that Jmmanuel was born as a JHWH, that is to say 'King of Wisdom.' A King of Wisdom is a human being who is knowledgeable and educated as high as possible in cognition, interpretation, and observance of the creational laws and recommendations and who strictly lives out the creational laws and recommendations.[56]

---

[53] Billy Meier, (2016. LVI), *Talmud of Jmmanuel*, Landesgruppe, Canada.

[54] Leon Levy, (2019, Document), *The Leon Levy Dead Sea Scrolls Digital Library*, accessed 1/11/2020, https://www.deadseascrolls.org.il/learn- about-the-scrolls/languages-and-scripts?locale=en_US.

[55] Billy Meier, (2016, 4), *Talmud of Jmmanuel*, Landesgruppe, Canada.

[56] Billy Meier, (2016, 18, 26, 52, 104), *Talmud of Jmmanuel*, Landesgruppe, Canada.

Therefore, there are portions of the Talmud of Jmmanuel that deal with UFO involvement with the extraterrestrials mating with Earth women, the extraterrestrial Gabriel mating with Mary, which resulted in the birth of Jmmanuel, the presence of a UFO, interpreted as a star, that led the wise men to Bethlehem, and several other appearances including the prophecy of the coming time when the presence of UFO will become more evident to humans on earth before there is "open contact" with mankind on Earth.[57]

Having said this, and sounding strange to your ears, it is really no different than reading strange happenings in the Bible that are expressed in archaic descriptions which could have been expressed in space technology language as in Ezekiel chapter 1 (KJV) where the wheels (UFO) that came down to Earth and a smaller wheel (UFO) separated from the larger wheel (UFO) and human-forms came out (aliens) and responded in the directional movement of the wheel (UFO). Another example of space technology language is found in Second Kings 2:11-12 (KJV) whereby Elijah boarded a spaceship and departed in it.

We have to remember that people in Biblical times, and before, described people, circumstances and events in the vocabulary that they knew and spoke at that time. Their descriptions for the most part was simple in their way of thinking. Their dictionary would be a lot smaller "in their day "compared to what it is today.

Suppose you keep an open mind to the transition of the times, yet keep the relevancy of UFO down through history. In that case, you will begin to see how alien technology and visitations are part of Biblical happenings.

---

[57] Pleune, D.R.E., (2019). *The Chariots Flew Then and Still Do Today.* Conneaut Lake, PA: Page Publishing, Inc. 19-21.

# Chapter 3

# The Evidence of Our Ancestry

When I speak to individuals or a group at a Community Education Program, Library, or Senior Center, I find that many state that they have seen a UFO... and even believe they exist. But when discussing the heritage/ancestry of man based on ufology, they back away. Why? The Christian religion has convinced them that the recording of creation and man's activities are God created and God directed. The evidence of extraterrestrial influence on mankind in the world does not seem to sink into their brain. In the past several thousands of years, the comprehension of recorded events has been short-circuited because of gene manipulation.

Those that are of a conservative religious conviction do not watch TV programs on ufology; it's all science fiction to them. They claim it is of the devil. Those that read of UFO or associated events look at it as though it is someone's opinion and therefore not reliable or credible. Ufology is not of prime importance to them because it doesn't fit into the scheme of their plans, aspirations, or convictions... therefore, of no relevance. Then there is what I call the "fringe religionist" that will be somewhat open to the idea of UFOs and possibly a credible presence from time to time on earth. A typical response of people of that notion is "Well, God created everything, and since there are so many stars in the sky, I would guess there is a possibility of life on at least a few of them." At this point, they back away for fear of ridicule, and they refuse to research the truth through the website *theyfly.com*.

In my previous book, "The Chariots Flew Then And Still Do Today," I point out the many proofs of alien activity in years past, such as drawings, carvings, and paintings in a Mexican Cave, a Mayan inscription at a stepped pyramid that says that it was a spot where the **ancient gods** visited from the heavens." As far away as Australia, there are stories of the Wandjina (sky-beings) that came down from the Milky Way. The Dogon tribe in West Africa tells the story of people from the Sirius system called Nommos who visited Earth thousands of years ago. In the U.S., there are accounts of Hopi Indian ancestors from the Pleiades. Other Native American tribes speak of the same or similar ancestry from those that came from a distant star, such as the Dakota Indians, Cree, Lakota, Zuni, and Apache Indians.[58]

Staying with ufology and the Plejarens from the Pleiades, we find their documentation of where various **races** came from. This subject is not dealt with anywhere in the Bible and is one of the first questions I had asked when first introduced to the Billy Meier and Plejaren accounts!!!

## How Races and the God of Religions Came About

A group of our Lyran ancestors settled on Earth and created the YETI,[59] a strange mixture of man's genetics. Many are still alive today because of very long-life spans. Today there are seven left in good hiding.

The White Race- The ancient Lyrans, a constellation between Hercules and Cygnus containing the bright star Vega. The ancient Lyrans were titans, standing 20 to 30 feet tall, from a planet much greater in size

---

[58] Billy Meier, "Contact 7, line 146," *They Fly*, February 25, 1975, http://www.theyfly.com/.

[59] Billy Meier, "Contact 236, line 191-193," *They Fly*, April 26, 1990. http://www.theyfly.com/.

than ours. They were white-skinned, with blond hair, usually had blue eyes, and had a life span of around 2,000 years.[60]

The Blue Race- Living underground for many years, a race of blue-skinned people has sometimes appeared. This race has two cities: one in France and one in Asia. They rarely come to the surface.[61]

The Black Race- 30,000 B.C. According to the "Chronological History of Mankind," the black race comes from Sirius." Sirius is the brightest star in the sky after the sun in the constellation Canis Major.[62]

The Red Race- Red, Brown, and white peoples.[63]

The Brown Race from the 70th Contact, Jan. 6, 1977- Coming from the north, the Son of Arus, Arus the 2nd, started a war and attacked those lands which are called today India, Pakistan, Persia, etc., where they met with the Sumerians, who, peace-loving, fled and vanished so far to the south, a nation of dark-colored skin, not negroid, but Europid and tall growth, risen from a race of Sirians. The latter had settled on the Earth some 33,000 years ago, synchronous with the refugees from the Pleja-System.[64]

---

[60] Billy Meier, "Contact 7, line 115," *They Fly*, February 25, 1975, http://www.theyfly.com/.

[61] Billy Meier, "Contact Report 5. February 16, 1975. http://semjase.net/semjeng6.html. Reviewed and corrected by Christian Frehner, administrator for Billy Meier, 11/7/2018.

[62] Billy Meier, "Contact 236, line 191-193," *They Fly*, April 26, 1990. http://www.theyfly.com/.

[63] Billy Meier, "Contact 70, line 131," *They Fly*, January 6, 1977. http://www.theyfly.com/.

[64] Billy Meier, "Contact 236, line 196," *They Fly*, April 26, 1990. http://www.theyfly.com/.

The brown (strongly dark-skinned) established in Africa and spread to Australia and New Zealand, and other locations.[65]

The yellow peoples- the Chinese and the Japanese- are the youngest inhabitants of the Earth because their appearance on this planet was only a little more than one cosmic age ago, and indeed, seemingly precisely 25,978 years ago.[66]

Within the vast time frame mentioned in the Chronology of Earth History is the account of the Sumerians, consisting of the people in the countries of Turkey, Iran, and Iraq, because it is the birthplace of Abraham, who is a major player in the Christian, Jewish and Muslim faiths. Details of the background on Abraham, family and faith are documented in my book "The Chariots Flew Then and Still Do Today."[67]

What is to be focused on is the role that extraterrestrials played thousands of years ago when it comes to identifying a "God" or "Gods," as in the case of Christianity whereby Biblical Scripture specifically identifies Jesus (Jmmanuel) as being God.

In doing so, we must understand that putting specific dates on events is hard to do when you do research back in the Old Testament. Instead of using dates, many events were couched in the form of such-and-such happening in the year of the reign of a king or a major event happening. This means there could be a large discrepancy of time that someone has relied on for teaching or learning but in great error due to unreliable or questionable assumptions such as dating events in the Old Testament based on genealogies of the Bible.

---

65  Ibid. 197.

66  Pleune, D.R.E., (2019, 66-92) *The Chariots Flew Then and Still Do Today.* Conneaut Lake, PA: Page Publishing, Inc.

67  Ibid. 88-90.

*Dr. Ron Pleune*

In my book, "The Chariots Flew Then and Still Do Today," I reveal the errors in using genealogies for dating Old Testament Biblical history, the real cause and time of the Noah Flood, the REAL God-leadership of the Hebrews, and much more. **We have a more accurate calendar that the Plejaren** from Erra have kept and now revealed to mankind on Earth, as stated in the Billy Meier story on theyfly.com. I urge you to check this topic out.[68]

An example of such a great discrepancy is the long-time assumption that the Noah Flood took place about 3,200 to 3,600 BC. Yet, the Plejaren have records of a gigantic comet, called the Destroyer Comet," that came by Earth every 575.5 years, and in 8,104 BC came by Earth super close and created the "world flood" as well as changed the axis of the earth and the length of the day.[69] There are even records on earth that prove the same!!!

However, in reading the Chronology of Earth History earlier in this work, it would <u>not</u> appear that the Destroyer Comet came exactly every 575.5 years after the year 8104 BC because the math does not support such a claim consistently. An explanation is as follows.

Christian Frehner, one of the Core Group members for Billy Meier, explains that the Destroyer Comet "has great intermediate fluctuations up to 205 years, which means that during a few rounds by the mutual gravitational attraction force of various planets, the sun and itself, its orbital period drops up to 478 years, respectively, and increases up to 683 years, but after a few rounds the constant orbital period returns to 575.5 years…which is very mysterious." Frehner goes on to say that "there is no need to fear the Destroyer Comet coming into our Solar System again because the Plejaren have deflected it" (Frehner 2019, email).

---

[68] Ibid. 66-73

[69] Walton, Travis, (1996), *Fire in The Sky*. 2nd Edition. Boston, Massachusetts, Da Capo Press, chapter 3.

This explanation by Mr. Frehner is borne out in the fact that as time continued from 8104 BC, the average time frame of the Destroyer Comet's appearance was rectified and proven in the "lesser flood" of 3453 BC, which scientists erroneously label as the "Noah Ark Flood."

**One of the greatest records on Earth of a Biblical God that was in actuality a highly intelligent extraterrestrial is in the history of the Hebrews as documented in the Sumerian King List and augmented with Biblical references.**

We first note that the lengths of reign of each of the Kings are unimaginable. Yet, the Plejaren in the Billy Meier story are 3,500 years ahead of us and have revealed that presentday Plejaren live up to 1,000 years of age. Living that long, or longer, seems unreal, but why? We tend to think and develop opinions in the context of what we know today rather than being open-minded to what has taken place in extraterrestrial life. We put ourselves in a box and close the lid, thinking that that is all that is known to man.

Think back to the time that the TV program *Star Trek* was aired. People thought it was really super to see humans transported in the "Transporter" room from the Starship Enterprise to the surface of a planet, and then back to the ship. Yet today, it is a reality as Billy Meier has experienced many times…and even a few documented abduction cases where people have been teleported from earth into a ship and later back to earth, as in the case of Travis Walton.[70] So, in reality, why is it so strange to think that extraterrestrial humans have lived so long in the past…and maybe yet today, which we have yet to discover? After all, think of Methuselah, who lived 969 years (Genesis 5:27 KJV).

---

[70] *The Billy Meier Story*. Directed by Jack Gerlach and Michael Horn. (2011); Laughlin, Nevada: Reality Films, DVD.

Dr. Ron Pleune

## They Were Here- And They Still Are

The (extraterrestrials- that is to say, humans of high technological intelligence) are beyond comprehension and further demonstrated in August 2016 when my wife and I began to use light signaling to summon UFOs. They would fly about 400 ft. above us, all lit up and then disappear after passing over. This is what Billy Meier called "Blinking." It is described by Semjase as an appearance of a UFO which then disappears and then re-appears in a different area of the sky. This phenomenon can be seen in the film *The Billy Meier Story* 2011, as filmed by Billy Meier himself.[71]

I also experienced the "Blinking" in and out of sight a UFO that looked exactly like Semjase's ship (one of the main teachers of Billy Meier), when on August 8, 2016, it hovered a few feet off the ground 300 ft. from my wife and me, in two 15 second views with about 10 seconds in between them. Each of the two events took place through the phenomenon of "Blinking" into view and then out of view.

Yes, extraterrestrial beings are here, but more unique than that is the fact that they have been coming and going from the earth and influencing our lives since 22 million BC, as shown previously on the "Chronology of the Earth."

A second verification of extraterrestrials coming to Earth is recorded in the King List from Sumeria. Their appearance was 241,200 years before the Noah Ark Flood in 8104 BC.[72]

When we think of "God" in the context of interpretation, we naturally think back to the Hebrews. But what does the word Hebrew have to

---

[71] Wikipedia s.v. (2019) "Sumerian King List," https://en.wikipedia.org/wiki/Sumerian_King_List

[72] Bernstein, Jeremy, (2013, Document.), *On Root/ What Does the Word "Hebrew" mean?* https://www.haaretz.com/israel-news/culture/premium-on-root-what-does-the-word-hebrew-mean- 1.5293110.

do with extraterrestrials? Or for that matter Abraham.... with "God" as an extraterrestrial?

We first have to understand what the word Hebrew means to understand these questions.

The greater portion of the Bible is written in Hebrew though the word is referred to in 2nd Kings 18 and Isaiah 36, where it is referred to as "Yehudit" which is to say "Judean." Hebrew today "yehudit" would mean "Jewish." In English, the word "Hebrew" points to two different things; the language and the people. The ethnic group, "ivri" does in fact appear in the Bible in Genesis 14, Exodus 1 and 2, and last Jonah.[73]

The Chambers Dictionary, 11th Ed. Lists the forms of the word Hebrew as Ebreu (French), Hebraenus (Latin), Hebraios (Greek), and 'ebrai (Heb. 'ibri') meaning 'one from the other side (of the Euphrates) or perhaps signifying "immigrant," noting as from a "region on the other or opposite side." Other sources agree i.e., the *Oxford English Dictionary 2nd*. Ed., and the *Etymonline and Collins English Dictionary*.[74]

The definition of "other side of the Euphrates," as well as "immigrant," are both fitting for the definition of the Hebrew people. When viewing a map of where Abraham's birthplace is, the city of Ur, it is located on the west bank of the Euphrates River. The question comes to mind of "what does the definition of the opposite side" have to do with the definition of Hebrew? Eventually Abraham went to Haran to the north, Genesis 11:31 (KJV), which is on the east side of the Euphrates River. This would validate the definition of Abraham being from the "other side" of the Euphrates.

Going back to the definition of Abraham and the Hebrew people, they were definitely "immigrants" as they sojourned from Ur to Haran,

---

[73] Ibid. Document.

[74] Billy Meier, "Contact 70, line 140-143," *They Fly*, January 6, 1977. http://www.theyfly.com/.

Egypt and eventually the land of Canaan Genesis 13:12 (KJV). Thus, the Billy Meier Contact Report#70 is right on target in describing who the Hebrew were…wandering, traveling and unsettled!! Thus, in Genesis 14:13 (KJV), the text specifically identifies Abraham for the first time as "Abraham the Hebrew."

Contact Report #70 refers to the Hebrews as a nation that was "none in itself" and was a widely disseminated alliance of gypsies (meaning wanderers, itinerant and unsettled ones) interspersed with spies and saboteurs of the then leader (God) Jehavon. The result was dissension everywhere (fights and quarrels), greed, robbery, arson, and murder. Thus, they were called Hebrews by the ancient language of their ancestors, known as Hebraons and later as the Hebrons. They were wanderers, traveling and unsettled.[75]

## The question comes back once again. WHO IS THE GOD OF THE HEBREW??

1) We need to keep in mind that the God (highly intelligent extraterrestrial) was present before Abraham.
2) The word "God" is a **title**, not a "personage."
3) The word "Lord," as in "Lord God," would refer to the "**position**" of God. This could be in the context of providing, directing, or doing something that would demonstrate a position of action and authority of that God.
4) A "**personage**" would refer to a specific God using their personal name such as the names of Gods that came to Earth in the Sumerian King List as well as the names of Gods that are listed in Contact Report #70 that lived and ruled for thousands of years.

---

[75] Wikipedia s.v. (2019) "Sumerian King List," https://en.wikipedia.org/wiki/Sumerian_King_List

An illustration of this can be seen at *https://en.wikipedia.org/wiki/Sumerian_King_List* where it states that the "kingship descended from heaven, the kingship was in Eridug." The spreadsheet documents 8 kings that reigned for varying lengths of time from the time they first came down from the Cosmos (referred to in the King List as Heaven), until the time of the Flood (which is the Noah Flood). These 8 kings reined a total of 241,200 years and then left Earth due to the total Earth Noahic flood.[76]

God (**his title**)- as one to be worshipped or revered.

Lord (**his position**)- as one that could change/produce/rule over.

Alulim (**his personage**) is referred to by a specific name/identity. In this case Alulim was the first one to come from heaven (cosmos) to rule.

What does the list tell us that we can learn from?

1) The kings came in an airship from the cosmos.
2) The kings were of a special breed and lived long lives (a capability of their ET origination).
3) The kings had the ability through an airship to leave Earth, as in the case of them leaving before the flood.

It is important to remember that the JHWH/IHWH (pronounced Ishwish), defined as King of Wisdom or a God, that the Hebrew experienced, were not the only ones to experience a "God" from the distant stars of the Universe, but there were others such as those that experienced a "God" in 11,000 B.C. A group of ETs of unknown origin arrive, led by a leader named Viracocoha, who controlled the city of Tiahuanaco. His base was on an island named Mot. He provided the inhabitants of Easter Island the tools to build the strange statues there

---

[76] Billy Meier, "Contact 69, part 1," *They Fly*, December 10, 1976, http://www.theyfly.com/.

which represent him and listed in the "Chronology of Earth History" earlier in this work.[77]

Another JHWH/IHWH, King of Wisdom or God, was the person known as Atlant who built the city of Atlantis.[78]

Still another extraterrestrial of high intelligence that was venerated as a God by the Aztecs was the one known as Quetzalcoatl.[79]

## What about God?

In conclusion, the God of the Hebrew people was whatever IHWH/JHWH/King of Wisdom that ruled over the Hebrew people at the time that the IHWH/JHWH/King of Wisdom existed until death, overthrown or left Earth to their home planet or another system.

But what about the God that supposedly created all things as spoken in Genesis chapter 1? The answer was given earlier in this writing but bore repeating once again.

The father of Semjase, Ptaah, clarifies the question as to who God is in Contact Report 32.

From Ptaah: (Semjase's father): Contact #32, lines 344-346.

344. The Creation however is the vastest, the almightiest and the glory itself.

---

[77] Billy Meier, "Contact 70, line 112- 113," *They Fly*, January 6, 1977. http://www.theyfly.com/.

[78] Billy Meier, "Contact 55, line 174-176," *They Fly* June 14, 1976. http://www.theyfly.com/.

[79] Billy Meier, "Contact 32, line 344-346," *They Fly*, September 8, 1975, http://www.theyfly.com/.

345. Through various circumstances, and not least through the megalomania of the human creatures, were JHWH/IHWHs, kings of wisdom, leaders of the people and leaders of the human race, **which according to Earth human terms were known as GOD, pressed into the term-related form of a Creator, and deceitfully declared as the highest in the Universe, namely the Creation itself.**

346. This is still evident today on the addressing form of the Earth humans, when they refer to their GOD as the CREATOR.[80]

Humans from corners of the universe that had the knowledge, skill, scientific know-how, and leadership abilities have always been egotistic, as seen in Contact Reports# 70, and #251. The society of mankind in the world today is no different. We see governments that are power-hungry and eager to launch verbal and physical war threats on other people of the Earth. Why? Because of gene manipulation from thousands of years ago… we still carry those traits as mentioned earlier in this work.

It is evident in our family lives with the discord, lack of understanding, the idea that "they personally" are right and everyone else is wrong. They push and shove their ideologies and greed for popularity and followers in social media to pump up their ego and their position in society as being idols to be worshiped by the coming generations. It is one thing to be an "idol," and it is quite another to be an "example." To be an "idol" is to be worshiped and adored with all the social "bling" that goes with it. To be an "example" is to live a positive life in all ways, not a show-off.

One who is an "example" speaks and conducts their life in such a way that honesty, modesty, truthfulness, and the virtues of love, peace, and harmony are their trophies…not money, rings, trophies, and titles; major on those things in life that help mankind, not pump up your ego like the highly scientific egos of alien humans that were considered Gods in the past.

---

[80] Ibid. 324-329.

This question is at the "crux" of what Christianity and all other religions that espouse to a monotheistic, dualistic or trinity Godhead because the falsehood of a God (in the human mind) signifies a central creator/Godhead and director of all things. The truth lies in the experience and records of the Cosmic Storage Banks.

The whole matter of God, a Savior, heaven, hell, angels and devils had its beginning millions of years ago through aliens that performed gene manipulation to humans on designated planets and brought to earth as well as gene manipulation that took place on earth by highly advanced alien scientists. Gene manipulation was covered previously in this work but the effects in the daily lives of Earth mankind will continue to plague us until scientists find the route to reverse the gene manipulation.

In review, mankind on Earth has been controlled by alien humankind who were identified as "God" or in the case of multiple highly advanced alien scientists, as "Gods." I refer you to the records of the Sumerian King List as well as Contact Report #32,# 70, and #251.

Semjase, one of the main teachers from the planet Erra, stated to Billy Meier the following regarding religion in the numbered lines as follows:[81] "324. So, when the terrestrial religions are spoken of negatively through Semjase, what is being addressed were and are the distortions and lies which are built into the religions, partly in a consciously deceitful way." (This is in reference to the gene manipulation by extraterrestrials held as Gods discussed previously). "325. By this however, are also addressed those sheer human, infamous concoctions, which you commonly have known as heresies and dogmas; sheer infamous concoctions by irresponsible or mistaken Earth humans, which through these heresies they have started, are able to beat your entire humanity into consciousness-based poverty and servitude. 326. The terrestrial religions are religions only in name because they are not such, but only cultic degenerations in a very evil sense. 327. Religions in this form are always false and deadly. 328. In reality, they should not be called religions

---

[81] Ibid. 407.

but cults. 329. In your case, we call them cultic religions because real religion-related facts are interspersed with cultic dogmas and heresies and adulterated."

Semjase goes on to state the process beginning in line# 345 that it began with those aliens identified by Earth humans as Gods. "345. Through various circumstances, and not least through the megalomania of the human creatures, were IHWHs, kings of wisdom, leaders of the people and leaders of the human race, which according to Earth human terms were known as GOD, pressed into the term-related form of a Creator, and deceitfully declared as the highest in the Universe, namely the Creation itself. 346. This is still evident today on the addressing form of the Earth humans, when they refer to their GOD as the CREATOR. 347. The masculine concept of HE and HIM and THE GOD could not, over many thousands of years, be expunged by the religious leaders. Consequently, this term still bears witness on Earth today, of the humanity of god and creator and the gods. 348. The Earth human however, in his thoughtless stupidity and in his unwillingness to surrender to the truth, has for a long time been unable to think about these things. 349. Insolently he continues to defend the cultic religions, which without exception are linked to some Earth humans and to a heavenly godhead."

To compound the religious idiocy of terrestrial humanity, extraterrestrial visitors on occasion have chosen to appear in such a way that they are viewed as emissaries of the Christian God. Semjase emphatically states the following on this matter as follows with line 407.[82]

"407. Aware of the religious power, they also do not shy away from posing as angels and messengers of God, and to appear as "saviors" of the humanity, wherein they then choose the deceived gullible ones for educational contacts, and assign them secret missions, which allegedly would serve the interests of the terrestrial humanity, but which in reality

---

[82] Ibid. 318-321.

*Dr. Ron Pleune*

only serve their own profit and the interests of the espionage of their own country."

Many people have said that God is known throughout the Universe when in fact, religion is only known on this Earth. Semjase states to Billy Meier the following regarding religion, beginning with line 318. "318. Religions in the sense that they exist on Earth, are actually unique in the span of the Universe known to us, and we don't find anything similar anywhere else. 319. As deadly threats, the false religions rule over the Earth humans and therefore the whole planet, and for thousands of years have let **your world atrophy** in consciousness-related terms. 320. Each consciousness-related advance is **blocked through these religions** and finds no further development. 321. The consciousness evolution and therefore also the spiritual evolution of the Earth humans are hampered through the false teachings of the religions."[83] (Bold print added for emphasis).

## Gene Manipulation

As stated previously in this work, the world struggles daily with the effects of gene manipulation.[84] "The genetically- manipulated people have since established themselves on Earth to the degree where they simultaneously became this planet's rulers and its destroyers, because most of them remained overly entangled in the effects of the manipulated genes of fighting, viciousness, barbarism, bloodthirstiness, greediness, addiction, emotionalism, inhumanities, to name but a few."

Doctrinally, mankind has suffered the lies that have come from what has been called the "original sin." Ptaah, Semjase's father, stated it this

---

[83] Billy Meier, "Contact 251, pg.4-25," *They Fly*, February 3, 1995. http://www.theyfly.com/.

[84] Ibid.

way in Contact Report 251.[85] "These characteristics have been an evil legacy for mankind from early times, and they also may actually be called **the "original sin."** Information regarding the "original sin" was **erroneously handed down by Christian religions** as the fable of **Adam, Eve, and the devilish snake in the Garden of Eden**. This "**original sin**," however, the genetic manipulation, repeatedly let the obsession for fighting and evil to surface from time immemorial- almost becoming Evil itself. Yet, in fact, this entire matter is based upon the manipulation of a single DNA gene that can be rectified if only our geneticists were to finally discover it."

Originally, Genetic Manipulation was used by one of the Lyran groups who had lost their ability to fight and wanted to "breed new human races" that were more able to fight. The new life forms from Genetic Manipulation ended up with barbaric traits that demonstrated "degeneration and cruelty" as well as a much shortened life span of approximately 100 years. The short story is that the two groups that had previously split eventually found their way to Earth, Malona, and Mars.

Over time, a comet named "The Destroyer" came by and destroyed Malona, made Mars uninhabitable, and led to the dominance of the "over-lords" on Earth. "**In this manner, the 'creator-overlords' were then capable of putting on the airs of terrestrial Man's creators** and, rising to power and **spreading their insane religious doctrines** which, however, contained an absolutely novel yet equally false history of humankind's origin, history, and belief. Its purpose was to definitively destroy and lose all data of mankind's true descent in the event that someone else would attempt to secretly glean the information from somewhere."[86]

---

[85] Billy Meier, "Contact 251, p.4-11," *They Fly*, February 3, 1995, http://www.theyfly.com/.

[86] Billy Meier, "Contact 70, line 153," *They Fly*, January 6, 1977, http://www.theyfly.com/

This should shed some light on the fact that we, terrestrial humans, were originally not so selfish, greedy, and eager for war, along with many other negative attributes.... not because of our own doing! Understand this clearly....no one was born in "sin." **We are a product of gene manipulation and wrong religious teachings of madness and cults** (bold print added), and many kinds of other evil machinations by former extraterrestrials,[87] and "By this, however, are also addressed those sheer human, infamous concoctions, which are commonly known as heresies and dogmas; **sheer infamous concoctions by irresponsible or mistaken Earth humans**, which through these heresies they have started, are able to beat your entire humanity into consciousness-based poverty and servitude" (Meier, line 325) (bold print added). [88]

Contact Reports 32, 70, and 251 open our eyes to the fact that not only did the gene manipulations negatively affect us physically but mentally in making us so that we are not able to remember our Ur (beginning) ancestry. Gene manipulation also affected us down through thousands of years in shortening the length of our physical lives and the way we interact in our social lives.

One of Billy's teachers, by the name of Ptaah (the father of Semjase), explains how man is saddled with genetic manipulation from thousands of years ago by God/Gods of alien form as follows.[89]

Beginning with line *124*... "124. This is indeed the case because whole numbers of serious and most serious diseases that appear in humanity on Earth have been programmed in a genetically manipulated form. 125. In order to free oneself from this, however, the humanity of Earth

---

[87] Billy Meier, "Contact 32, line 325," *They Fly*, September 8, 1975, http://www.theyfly.com/.

[88] Billy Meier, "Contact 252, line 124-126," *They Fly*, February 14, 1995. http://www.theyfly.com/.

[89] Billy Meier, "Contact 002, line 24-30," *They Fly*, February 3, 1975. http://www.theyfly.com/.

or its scientists must learn how to deal with genetic manipulation, for which we release impulses in a responsible manner. 126. However, the path of development will be very long, because the research and the successes resulting from it must not overflow so that damage is not done again."

Religious stories, customs, and worship mandates were introduced that kept mankind under submission, such as the truth about the genealogy of Jmmanuel, the virgin birth, baptism, raising a person from the dead, and other events known as miracles.

## Impulse (Impulse-Telepathic Nature)

A word about "impulses" as mentioned above. Impulses and mental telepathy are two different subjects. In mental telepathy, there can be a conversation of sorts from a human to an alien. In Billy Meier's case, he conducted conversation with his various alien teachers through mental telepathy due to the discussion of matters. They are not allowed to penetrate the thoughts of humans because it is not their desire, nor do they feel that they have a right to the personal secrets of people.[90] This is also confirmed by Billy's contact prior to Semjase by the name of Asket, who is from the DAL Universe, a parallel Universe from our present Universe, which is called the DERN Universe.[91]

Impulses are quite different. Impulses are like "hints" given to humans from aliens that transmit from their mind to ours. They are not conversations but a brief word or sudden thought that will suddenly answer a question that results in an action such as when a person is inventing something and is puzzled about how to proceed. Semjase, an instructor of Billy, confirmed the "impulse-telepathic" mode of helping

---

[90] Billy Meier, "Asket's Explanations- Part 1, line 116, *They Fly*, February 3, 1953, http://www.theyfly.com/.

[91] Billy Meier, "Contact 003, line 19," *They Fly*, February 8, 1975, http://www.theyfly.com/.

those with technical inventions;[92] Ptaah, which is another teacher of Billy's and also the father of Semjase,[93] affirms the impulse-telepathic process,[94] by specifically agreeing with Billy that these <u>impulses that are telepathic</u> have been transmitted to terrestrial researchers, scientists, and engineers in the past.

Further confirmation of "impulses" that are transmitted to humans can be found in the 544th Contact Report, where Ptaah, who is the father of Semjase, states the following to Billy Meier.

"With certain humanities, therefore, we are to endeavor, to teach inconspicuous persons through impulses of universally identical creative-natural laws and recommendations, so that these ones, in a teaching-like way, can take action with their peoples, however without having any idea of the fact that impulse-like instructions have been given to them."[95]

---

[92] Billy Meier, "Contact 249, pg. 1," *They Fly,* June 13, 1994, http://www.theyfly.com/.

[93] Billy Meier, "Contact 567, pg. 1," *They Fly,* July 6, 2013, http://www.theyfly.com/.

[94] Billy Meier, "Contact 544, line 47," *They fly,* July 13, 2012: http://www.theyfly.com/.

[95] Billy Meier, "Contact 006, line 28," *They Fly*, February 23, 1975, http://www.theyfly.com/.

# Chapter 4

# Biblical Issues

## Heaven and Hell- the Religion Seduction

The ignorance of religious teachings continues today in which religious colleges, seminaries, missionary indoctrination, church school, Sunday school, catechisms, Bible camps, Christian retreats, and a host of Christian publications influence the thinking of people that God and a Savior are the way to salvation and eternal life. Yet the Plejaren, who we can read about in the Billy Meier contact notes, have spoken of the proof that there is no heaven or hell because they have searched the universe and found that these places do not exist.

Semjase, a major teacher of Billy Meier, states, "…hell, in truth, means nothing other than a self-inflicted punishment that must be served…" [96]

".liberators (angels). the shadow world (hell) or into heaven.they are inventions of your own without any power and without any existence and reality…" [97]

---

[96] Billy Meier, *Goblet of the Truth*. (Canada: FIGU-Landsgruppe Canada, 2015, 55).

[97] Billy Meier, *Goblet of the Truth*. (Canada: FIGU-Landsgruppe Canada, 2015, 77).

Dr. Ron Pleune

"...therefore, there are neither gods nor tin gods, nor people of your kind (human beings) or liberators (angels) and demons that stand above it..." [98]

Additional information regarding the non-existence of Heaven or Hell given to Billy Meier through the Plejaren in the "Goblet of the Truth" is as follows in multiple pages listed.[99]

|  | Pg. | Ch. | V. |
|---|---|---|---|
| Heaven- a state of inner being made by yourself | 207 | 6 | 71 |
| Heaven- is false and just an invention by those in delusion which puts people in bondage of thoughts | 57 | 2 | 326 |
| Heaven- is not a place but rather condition in yourselves | 499 | 28 | 49 |
| Heaven- false teachings and fundamentally wrong | 499 | 28 | 49 |
| Heaven- is within you | 171 | 5 | 32 |
| Heaven- is within you | 455 | 25 | 203 |
| Hell- is within you | 171 | 5 | 32 |
| Hell- is within you when your inner world goes/feels wrong | 455 | 25 | 203 |
| Hell- a shadow world "hell on earth" due to allowing belief in a god or tin gods and affecting your psyche and life | 75 | 3 | 14 |

---

[98] Billy Meier, *Goblet of the Truth*. (Canada: FIGU-Landsgruppe Canada, 2015, (multiple pages).

[99] Billy Meier, (2016), *Talmud of Jmmanuel*. Chapter 4, verses 50-52. FIGU-Landsgruppe, Toronto, Canada.

| | | | |
|---|---|---|---|
| Hell- created within if you hold to pretexts and cowardice by refusing to change | 383 | 21 | 30 |
| Hell- a shadow world within yourself when you refuse to turn to the Truth | 239 | 7 | 42-43 |
| Hell- false teachings and fundamentally wrong | 499 | 28 | 49 |
| Hell- no such place in a religious context where a devil and human punishment exist | 329 | 11 | 65-66 |
| Hell- is not a place but rather condition in yourselves | 499 | 28 | 49 |
| Hell- (a shadow world) unfair ones accuse the true prophets of activities of the shadow world (hell) | 201 | 6 | 37 |
| Hell- a state of inner being made by yourself | 207 | 6 | 71 |
| Hell- depravity from within | 115 | 3 | 243 |
| Hell- a shadow world that destroys you through unrighteousness | 159 | 4 | 215 |
| Hell- (a shadow world) what you create inside yourself when you do evil toward others | 233 | 7 | 19 |
| Hell- self-created shadow world by a person's own decision | 147 | 4 | 147 |
| Hell- imaginary, created through your thoughts and feelings and result in evil deeds | 439 | 25 | 103 |
| Hell- a shadow world created within you when you refuse the Truth | 185 | 5 | 94 |
| Hell- a shadow world when NOT creating knowledge, love, freedom, pace& harmony | 149 | 4 | 157 |

*Dr. Ron Pleune*

| | | | |
|---|---|---|---|
| Hell- is a shadow world and does not exist; it is a condition of your feeling | 27 | 2 | 175 |

| | | | |
|---|---|---|---|
| Hell- a shadow world created within you when you have hostility toward the Truth | 293 | 9 | 60-63 |
| Hell- a shadow world you live in when you are hypocritical | 295 | 9 | 68 |
| Hell- a shadow world within you when living in hypocrisy and a loveless life | 295 | 9 | 73 |
| Hell- shadow world created by unknowledgeness and rejection of the Laws and Recommendations | 187 | 5 | 108 |
| Hell- a shadow world when persisting in unknowledgeness of the Truth | 143 | 4 | 127 |
| Hell- a shadow world through destroying nature, war, hatred, jealousy, revenge, retaliation & all evil | 235 | 7 | 25 |
| Hell- a shadow world created when a person persists in unknowledgeness & rejects the signs (evidence) of the Laws & Rec.'s | 187 | 5 | 108 |
| Hell- the shadow world created by you and within you | 169 | 5 | 23 |
| Hell- is only created in your life by bad deeds | 115 | 3 | 239 |
| Hell- a condition within that can be changed with the rightness of the Truth | 273 | 8 | 37 |
| Hell- a shadow world in you when not creating knowledge, love, wisdom & resulting in no freedom, no peace and no harmony | 149 | 4 | 157 |

| | | | |
|---|---|---|---|
| Hell- fabulated by humans and an evil condition created in you by you | 171 | 5 | 32 |
| Hell- occurs due to evil within | 239 | 7 | 42 |
| Hell (fire)- does not exist; invented delusion to coerce humans to follow false God (s) and servants | 53 | 2 | 304 |
| Hell (fire)- a threat used by those (God believers) that reject the Truth | 111 | 3 | 230 |
| Hell (fire)- it is not reality, just an internal feeling in accordance with your own deeds, efforts, and blame (responsibility) | 115 | 3 | 239 |

Let me challenge the mind of mankind and say this:

1. Since there are alien humans that have visited our Earth for thousands and thousands of years, they have never stated that there is a God or divine/heavenly entity or entities.

2. God (s) or Sub-God (s) of divine nature are never proven, only "cloaked" as being divine because they (the alien humans) have considered the highly intelligent and scientific alien humans to be called God (s).

3. Humans of today that flatly deny the existence or state that there "probably" are alien entities in the universe but go no further in the research of the topic to confirm that they exist, such as through the Billy Meier accounts of the Plejaren existing (of which some have witnessed their presence in the existence of their ship (s)), serves only to promote their own ignorance.

4. Even with the confirmation by astronauts seeing alien entities in our atmosphere as well as on the moon, there are still those that do not believe in UFOs.

5. More and more UFO film and account documentation are being revealed from the past and recorded in the present through various media outlets.

6. Mankind is ignorant as it is with their religiosity. Once again, this goes back to confirming the gene manipulation and teachings of alien entities in the past of lies to a) cover up their own barbarism toward mankind and b) the made-up religious lies to put mankind under their servitude through false teachings of doctrine.

7. Continued ignorance, or should I put it more aptly "stupidity," of mankind will come home to roost one day when alien entities will visit us more often as told in the scrolls found in 1963 called the Talmud of Jmmanuel where it states in Chapter 4:50-52.[100] Hence, following the fulfillment of your calling (mission), there will be a time of many hundreds and, thus, two times a thousand years and more before the truth of the knowledge you brought among the people will be recognized and disseminated by a few human children. Not until the time of firmament-rushing ships and chariots of fire (aircraft and rockets) will the truth break through- and thus, not until then will the falsified teaching of the truth confused by zealots (fanatics) gradually falter- that you are not the son of a god and are not the Creation, and you should not be worshipped as such. And this will be the time when we celestial sons reveal ourselves to the human species again in a new form and first only in hiddenness (secrecy), and only when the human beings have become knowing but even more astray from the truth and threaten the structure of the firmament (the universe) with their acquired might, will the time come for open encounterance (for open contact)."

This portion of Scripture tells us that as the days pass by, comprised of several hundred years plus two thousand years ( "many hundreds and,

---

[100] Billy Meier, "Contact 251, pg. 1-35," *They Fly*, February 3, 1995, http://www.theyfly.com/.

thus two times a thousand years and more") will pass before the correct teachings of the Truth of Jmmanuel (known to Christianity as Jesus) is accepted by mankind, that is to say, that "the truth breaks through" and that the Biblical message and account will be recognized as false.

My point is this, why remain ignorant as Harry S. did when I wrote of his flat denial of UFO existing…then of how he admitted to me of the existence of UFO in the experience he and his wife had in the upper peninsula of Michigan? The problem here is that Harry S. was such an honest man, and one that stated that UFO entities do not exist had to keep the experience he and his wife went through as a secret the rest of their lives! Why would Harry S. tell me of this experience and admit that he and his wife did not tell anyone of it except for telling me?

The answer lies in the fact it was to prepare me for what lay ahead in working with Billy Meier. I was a conservative Christian at the time, former pastor and evangelist!

Mentally I was not prepared to accept the reality of UFOs at that time! A year later, my wife at the time and I witnessed a UFO hovering about 500 ft. above our back yard on a cloudless day. George, a fellow employee, told me in the early 1980s of a UFO experience he and his wife had at one time... yet he told no one else just as Harry S. testified, once again preparing me for the time to come in working with Billy Meier. I was further being prepared (unknowingly) in 2014 when I picked up the book "Light Years" by Gary Kinder in, which I read through several times.

My present wife and I examined the contact reports of Billy Meier and all the proof that was recorded of the truth of his experience with the Plejaren from the Pleiades. In January/February of 2016, we left Christianity for the Truth revealed to Billy Meier. The prophecies were indisputable; the Goblet of the Truth written by Billy Meier as the last of the seven prophets gave us freedom from all the trappings of

Christianity and the many false stories and doctrine of the Christian faith that came from the Bible.

<u>As 2016 moved along, I proposed to Billy Meier that I would like to develop an index to the Goblet of the Truth. This index would list all the subjects dealt with from within the Goblet of the Truth. A few days later, his head administrator informed me that Billy gave his o.k. and that I would work with a man in California to set up the spreadsheet for such an endeavor. Over three and a half years later, I am still entering subjects from the Goblet of the Truth onto the Index of the Goblet of the Truth.</u>

Our UFO contact efforts have continued with many great experiences from simple exchanges of light signaling from us to UFO and them back to us, to summoning a ship on February 17, 2017, that was approximately 250 ft. in diameter that hovered approximately 500 ft. above the small town of Orleans, Michigan, at about 7:35 p.m. An adult niece of mine and I observed the UFO and 12 other small UFO hovering around it for 25 minutes.

The Billy Meier story is not all about UFO; it also concerns learning how to live in love, peace, freedom, and harmony with other humans in spite of the genetic manipulations that each of us have had to endure for so many thousands of years ago and passed down through our ancestry to present day. One of the greatest learning tools has been the Goblet of the Truth which gives us guidance in learning and understanding why we are the way we are and learning the concepts of relating to one another without prejudice, hatred, and bias, as well as how to be positive and understanding. This will be covered later in this work.

## Original Sin/ Doctrine of Salvation

What are the doctrinal issues that have been taught and applied in the Christian Religion? One of them that have already been touched upon is the erroneous teaching of "original sin." In Christianity, the subject is claimed to originate as being passed down from Adam to all mankind due to the disobedience of Adam/Eve in the Garden of Eden (Romans 5:12 KJV) by eating of the fruit of "the tree of the knowledge of good and evil" (Genesis, chapter 2, KJV).

What a fantastic portion of Scripture in Genesis, chapter 3, (KJV), that confirms that there were other Gods at the time (as previously noted in this work under the topic of the Sumerian Gods as well as the Gods in their malicious lives that ended up ruling over the Hebrews. How do we get that fact? In Genesis chapter 3, verse 5, (KJV), it tells us that "in the day ye eat thereof, then your eyes shall be opened and **ye shall be as gods**, knowing good and evil."

This Scripture from the Bible is a "white-wash" to cover up the fact that the Gods at that time (thousands and thousands of years ago) performed gene manipulation and turned around and taught it in Christianity as "the original sin" because the highly intelligent scientific humans known as Gods did not want to bear the responsibility of such a horrific act that would remain in the human race until some day it would be discovered how to repair such a condition.

Not only that, but the same verse states that mankind would know good and evil, in other words knowing the difference between the two, which amounted to a risk that God and other Gods would face in the matter of controlling the human race. The Plejaren had confirmed in Contact #

251,[101] through Billy Meier repeating back to Ptaah the story of mankind on Earth, that "there is no such thing that Man is born evil in the sense that he or she is totally evil from birth onward, as some people enjoy claiming; those who wish only to see evil and total negativity. "[102]

---

101  Billy Meier, "Contact 251, pg. 9," *They Fly*, February 3, 1995, http://www.theyfly.com/.

102  Billy Meier, "Contact 251, pg. 7," *They Fly*, February 3, 1995, http://www.theyfly.com/.

The matter of "knowing good and evil" is summed up in where it is recorded as follows. "**As a result of these genetic manipulations, and from earliest times, Man has fought these inner conflicts of good and evil- where evil frequently is the winner. Nonetheless, increasing numbers of humans combat their way to goodness by conquering the damage done by genetic manipulation and their wicked legacy, i.e., the evil or original sin. Unfortunately, frequent excesses occur that are based upon degeneration and pseudo-humanism, because humans are unable to find the appropriate paths and cling to false ideals that frequently originated from religious-sectarian idiocy."**[103]

## Adam and Eve

In actuality, the Biblical story of Adam and Eve is incorrect as reported below. Semjase advised Billy Meier that "Semjasa, the highest leader of the sub-leaders, mated with an **EVA**, a female being, who was still mostly human-like and also rather beautiful (in feature and form). The descendent of this act was of male sex and a human being of good form. Semjasa called him "**ADAM**," which was a word meaning "Earth human being." Similar breeding produced a female, and in later years, they were mated to each other. Meanwhile, others similar had been produced who formed groups and tribes. From these, present (i.e., at that time) Earth mankind developed."[104]

## Sons of God Saw the Daughters of Men

A further demonstration of the cobbled-up stories in the Bible involves Genesis, chapter 6, verses 1- 4, (KJV). It speaks of people beginning to multiply on earth and that "the sons of god saw the daughters of men that they were fair; and they took them wives of all which they chose."

---

[103] Billy Meier, "Contact 9, pg. 2," *They Fly*, March 21, 1975, http://www.theyfly.com/.

[104] Ibid.

There has been a lot of conjecture about who these "sons of god" were, of which I am going to avoid the arguments about the topic and simply state the TRUTH as revealed in Contact Report #9.[105] You will note that Arus is mentioned in the following quote and is also referenced in the Chronology of Earth in Chapter 2 of this writing which will give you some background. "But centuries before this point <u>in time, the intruders boasted</u> of their conquest of Earth, and IHWH ARUS led a severe and bloody regime. Still, his sub-leaders assumed for themselves many things and became more and more independent. Within only three decades, they had gone far in their own decision-making, even though they feared the punishments of the IHWH ARUS. They advocated a codex, to under all circumstances maintain their own race and not allow it to fall to mutations away from themselves. In a forbidden manner and secretly, they went out and caught wild Earth creatures and mutations who were distant descendants of former human beings from cosmic space. Wild and beautiful female beings were tamed and mated with by the sub-leaders who called themselves "Sons of Heaven".

It can well be imagined that any religious leader is saying by now that this is a bunch of malarkey, and I can understand this because the religious community (speaking of Christianity and its many offshoots and branches, as well as independent Bible, associated systems) has their followers ground in what is being taught from their "religious" book. This is not an effort in "religion bashing," but it is a work in "religious awakening." I was blind to the Truth when I was in Christianity, but in asking questions about the dating of events, proof of events, how cataclysmic events took place through natural weather happenings or how geological happenings occurred through cosmic events, how miracles are in truth, nothing more than cause and effect, the natural process of nature and our body-healing, as well as the dying process at work that my eyes were opened to the revelations of our cosmic ancestry and the influence ufology, has had on mankind.

---

105  Pleune D.R.E, Ronald, (2019. 66-75) *The Chariots Flew Then and Still Do Today.* Conneaut Lake, PA: Page Publishing, Inc.

This whole matter has been previously explored through the influence of our ancestry with those that have come to Earth and influenced mankind to who and what they are today. The topic of how we deal with life and treat one another will be dealt with later in this writing when we look into the Goblet of the Truth.

## World Flood of Noah's Time

Still, another erroneous account in the Bible is the Noah Flood as recorded in the Bible in Genesis chapter 6, 7, and 8. The reason for the Flood in the Bible is because God was grieved over all the corruption of mankind, chapter 6, verses 11-13. God's remedy was to destroy mankind except for those aboard the ark. The story is a concocted lie... a natural cosmic event took place in 8104 B.C., as revealed by the Plejaren in the Chronology of the Earth that is presented earlier in this work.

The accurate details of the event are recorded in my previous book titled "The Chariots Flew Then and Still Do Today!" [106] The main source of information for the account of the Flood comes from and is summarized as follows.[107]

- \* The "Destroyer" Comet came super close to Earth in 8104 B.C. (10079 years from the time it was announced in Contact Report #5) which previously came near earth every 575.5 years.
- \* The number of hours in a day was shortened from 40+ hrs. to 24 hrs.
- \* The rotation direction of the Earth changed.

---

106  Billy Meier, "Contact 5, pg. 26-60," *They Fly*, February 16, 1975, http://www.theyfly.com/.

107  *Wikipedia*, s.v., "Biblical Literalist Chronology." last edited on 13 July 2018, (Accessed October 22, 2018), https://en.wikipedia.org/wiki/Biblical literalist chronolog y.

*God, The Grandest Illusion*

## Genealogies of the Bible

The genealogies in the Bible remain a hot topic because of those that choose a "young world" approach vs. an "old world approach." Those that choose to believe the "young world" approach hold tightly to one or a combination of the following such as "Archbishop James Ussher, who placed it in 4,004 BCE, Isaac Newton in 4,000 BCE, Martin Luther in 3,961 BCE, the traditional Jewish date of 3,760 BCE, and the traditional Greek Orthodox date, based on the Septuagint, of 5,009 BCE (Wikipedia, 2018)."[108]

Yet, the truth is revealed by the Plejaren regarding the Genealogy of Adam from the Storage Banks of the universe.[109] It is a document that was discovered in 1963 by Billy Meier and a former Greek-Orthodox priest by the name of Isa Rashid. Originally there were four rolls and translations which were in possession of Isa Rashid until Isa and his family fled from a refugee camp in Lebanon to another camp. The only translation that survived and sent to Billy Meier was through the Talmud of Jmmanuel's 36th chapter. Billy learned of the assassination of Isa Rashid, and his family took place in Baghdad in 1976. Some would say that the findings of such documents consisting of four scrolls is just a scam, yet within itself is the testimony of its age and the authenticity of its language (Meier, 2016, Forward LXXXIV-CXX).[110]

---

108  Billy Meier, *Talmud of Jmmanuel*, (2016. 18-24). Landesgruppe, Canada.

109  109-Billy Meier, *Talmud of Jmmanuel*, (2016. LXXXIV-CXX). Landesgruppe, Canada.

110  Billy Meier, (2016, 18-38), *Talmud of Jmmanuel*, Landesgruppe, Canada.

*Dr. Ron Pleune*

# The Talmud of Jmmanuel and the Genealogy of Jmmanuel

1. This is the book and Arcanum of Jmmanuel, who is called "the one with godly knowledge," who is the son of Joseph, grandson of Jacob, a distant descendant of David. David was a descendant of Abram (Abraham), whose genealogy traces back to Adam, the father of a lineage of terrestrial humans as follows.[111]

2. Adam was begotten by Semjasa, the leader of the celestial sons who were the guardian angels of god, the great ruler of the travelers from afar.

3. Semjasa, the celestial son and guardian angel of god, the great ruler of the voyagers who traveled here through vast expanses of the universe, took a terrestrial woman and begot Adam, the father of the white human population.

Adam took for himself an Earth wife and begot Seth. 4) Seth begot Enos. 5) Enos begot Akjbeel. 6) Akjbeel begot Aruseak. 7) Aruseak begot Kenan. 8) Kenan begot Mahalaleel. 9) Mahalaleel begot Urakjbarameel. 10)

Urakjbarameel begot Jared. 11) Jared begot Henoch. 12) Henoch begot Methusalah. 13) Methusalah begot Lamech. 14) Lamech begot Tamjel. 15) Tamjel begot Danel. 16) Danel begot Asael. 17) Asael begot Samsafeel. 18) Samsafeel begot Jomjael. 19) Jomjael begot Turel. 20) Turel begot Hamech. 21) Hamech begot Noah. 22) Noah begot Sem. 23) Sem begot Arpachsad. 24) Arpachsad begot Batraal. 25) Batraal begot Ramuel. 26) Ramuel begot Askeel. 27) Askeel begot Armers. 28) Armers begot Salah. 29) Salah begot Eber. 30) Eber begot Peleg. 31) Peleg begot Regu. 32) Regu begot Serug. 33) Serug begot Araseal. 34) Araseal begot Nahor. 35) Nahor begot Thara. 36) Thara begot Abraham. 37) Abraham begot Jsaak. 38) Jsaak begot Jacob. 39) Jacob begot Juda. 40) Juda begot Ananj. 41) Ananj begot Ertael. 42)

---

[111] Billy Meier, "Contact 009, pg. 1-2," *They Fly*, March 21, 1975, http://www.theyfly.com/.

*God, The Grandest Illusion*

Ertael begot Perez. 43) Perez begot Hezron. 44) Hezron begot Ram. 45) Ram begot Amjnadab. 46) Amjnadab begot Savebe. 47) Savebe begot Nahesson. 48) Nahesson begot Sahna. 49) Sahna begot Boas. 50) Boas begot Obed. 51) Obed begot Jesse. 52) Jesse begot David. 53) David begot Solomon. 54) Solomon begot Asa. 55) Asa begot Gadaeel. 56) Gadaeel begot Josaphat. 57) Josaphat begot I (J)ora. 58) I (J)ora begot Armeneel. 59) Armeneel begot Usja. 60) Usja begot Jothan. 61) Jothan begot Gadreel. 62) Gadreel begot Ahas. 63) Ahas begot Jtjskja. 64) Jtjskja begot Manasse. 65) Manasse begot amen. 66) Amen begot Josja. 67) Josja begot Jojachjn. 68) Jojachjn begot Sealthjel. 69) Sealthjel begot Jequn. 70) Jequn begot Serubabel. 71) Serubabel begot Abjud. 72) Abjud begot Eljakjim. 73) Eljakjm begot Asor. 74) Asor begot Zadok. 75) Azdok begot Achjm. 76) Achjm begot Eljud. 77) Eljud begot Eleasar. 78) Eleasar begot Matthan. 79) Matthan begot Jacob. 80) Jacob begot Joseph.

81) Joseph was the husband of Mary, the mother of Jmmanuel, who was impregnated by a distant descendant of the celestial son, Rasiel, who was the guardian angel of the secret.

82) When Joseph heard of Mary's secret impregnation by a descendant of the celestial sons from the lineage of Rasiel, behold, he was filled with wrath and thought of leaving Mary before he would be married to her before the people.

83) While Joseph was thinking in this manner, behold a guardian angel, sent by Gabriel, the celestial son who had impregnated Mary, appeared and said:

84) "Joseph, Mary is betrothed to you, and you are to become her spouse; do not leave her, because the fruit of her womb is chosen for a great purpose. Marry her in all openness so that you may be husband and wife before the people.

*Dr. Ron Pleune*

85) "Behold, the impregnation of Mary occurred eleven thousand years after the procreation of Adam through the celestial son Semjasa, to fulfill the word of god, the ruler of those who traveled from afar, who conveyed these words through the prophet Isaiah:

86) "Behold, a virgin will be impregnated by a celestial son before she is married to a man before the people.

87) "They will name the fruit of her womb Jmmanuel, which translated means 'the one with godly knowledge,' as a symbol and honor to god. Through god's power and providential care, the Earth was made to bear intelligent human life when the celestial sons, the travelers from the far reaches of the universe, mated with the women of Earth.

88) "Behold, god and his followers came far from the depths of space, where they delivered themselves from a strong bondage and created here a new human race and home with the early women of this Earth.

(The term "god" in the above references is actually what Christianity refers to as "The God" which is a mistaken identity for the highly intelligent/scientific humans from the universe as previously explained.)

The age of each individual is not recorded in the above genealogy, but we do know that humans from the Universe did indeed live very long lives. Several sources point this out.

* The King List of Sumeria that records individual kings living for thousands of years.

    The Chronology of the Earth, shown earlier, records Leaders of ET groups as living for several thousands of years.

    Semjase pointed out in Contact Report #9, that alien humans approximately 15,000 years ago had used mutation and their sciences to **extend their life spans to thousands of years.**[112]

---

[112] Billy Meier, "Contact 003, line 48-51," *They Fly*, February 8, 1975, http://www.theyfly.com/.

*God, The Grandest Illusion*

In the present modern times, Semjase (Billy's main teacher) states that their (Plejaren) "average life expectancy is about 1,000 years."[113]

* Wikipedia records, as unreliable in totality that they are, date the "anatomically modern humans, as of <u>2017, to be about 300,</u>000 years old." [114]

* Two fossil jaws <u>found recently</u> in Ethiopia suggest the human genus, *Homo*, arrived in East Africa around 2.8 million years ago. The <u>remains of Lucy,</u> a famous early human ancestor, indicate she roamed present-day Ethiopia 3.2 million years ago.[115]

## The Fiery Chariot

Still, another event that was due to the fact that the writer of the Scripture at the time did not understand the proper terminology for Ufological events. After all, their linguistic dictionary and customs at that time did not use the terminology we use today which I call *transinterpretate*.

Here is an example from 2 Kings 2:11 (KJV) that I pointed out in my previous book, *The Chariots Flew Then and Still Do Today!* The first word that needs to be *transinterpretated* is the word for chariot.[116] The word "chariot" first of all is not capitalized and in its general sense, is a

---

[113] *Wikipedia, s.v., David Richter et al. (8 June 2017). "The age of the hominin fossils from Jebel Irhoud, Morocco, and the origins of the Middle Stone Age". Nature.* **546** *(7657): 293-*

[114] Maria Gallucci. 2017. Document "This 400,000-year-old cranium offers new clues on human evolution" Accessed December 12, 2019. http://mashable.com/2017/03/13/human-fossil-evolution- portugal/#gj Dom4N4EqI.

[115] Pleune D.R.E., Ronald, (2019. 79-80) *The Chariots Flew Then and Still Do Today.* Conneaut Lake, PA: Page Publishing, Inc. 79-80.

[116] *Wikipedia s.v.,* "The Lost Books of the Bible." Document. (Accessed December 20, 2019). https://en.wikipedia.org/wiki/The Lost Books of the Bible and the Forgotten Books of Eden

mode of transportation. The second word of interest is the word "fire." At this point, it would raise a person's eyebrows if a chariot was on fire, but there is nothing in the verse to suggest that it was actually burning up and resulting in a pile of ashes. Now keeping that in mind, we approach another weird spectacle called "horses of fire." Keep in mind that scribes used what vocabulary was at hand, and when we look at the Hebrew meaning of horses of fire it is not to be translated in the context of actual horses, but "as the sound of horses" That is to say, the sound of a flying machine which would make the roar of horses running as if they were on fire or driven by fire. If these were actual horses with an actual open chariot, the riders and horses would never survive due to the eventual altitude and result in the passenger fainting and dying as well as the horses. The whirlwind at the end of the verse is simply the rush of air from engines that gave the spaceship propulsion for either vertical or horizontal ascent into the sky.

The verse now would read, "And it came to pass, as they still went on, and talked, that behold there appeared a space ship glowing as if on fire, and the loud sound of its engines was that of running horses that were driven by fire; Elijah then boarded the craft, and the ship departed with a rush of air from its engines into the sky."

There are many more topics that are false in whole or in part, but the main reason for covering the ones above is that they are usually topics that the general population responds with "but what about this or that?"

The information regarding the identity of God and the associated history should be a major step in correcting the concept that Christianity has for so long proclaimed as historically and divinely accurate…but is considerably incorrect in whole or in part.

*God, The Grandest Illusion*

## Inaccuracies, Contradictions, Fallacies, Scientific Issues

If you ask for the general topic of errors, inaccuracies, and flaws in the Bible, you will get a host of sites, as I have listed below.

1. *The Problem of the Bible: Inaccuracies, contradictions, fallacies, scientific issues and more.* https://www.news24. com/MyNews24/The- Problem-of-the-Bible-Inaccuracies- contradictions- fallacies-scientific-issues-and-more-20120517

2. *Biblical scientific errors- RationalWiki,* https://rationalwiki.org > wiki >Biblical scientific errors

3. *4 Informal Logical Fallacies& Biblical Examples-CrossExamined.org* https://crossexamined.org/4-informal-logical-fallacies- biblical-examples/

4. *Debunking Christianity: A Great List of Biblical Fallacies* www.debunking-christianity.com/2007/09/great- list-of-biblical-fallacies.html

5. *Some Reasons Why Humanists Reject the Bible* https://americanhumanist.org/what-is-humanism/reasons-humanists-reject-bible/

6. *The Problem of the Bible: Inaccuracies, contradictions, fallacies, scientific issues and more* https://www.debate.org/debates/The-Problem-of-the-Bible-Inaccuracies-contradictions-fallacies- scientific-issues-and-more./1/

7. *Biblical Contradictions* https://www.atheists.org/activism/resources/biblical-contradictions/

8. *A list of over 700 inconsistencies in the Bible* https://www.cs.umd.edu/~mvz/bible/bible- inconsistencies.pdf

9. *Top 20 Most Damning Bible Contradictions* **https://www.patheos.com/blogs/crossexamined/2018/10/top-20-most-damning-bible**-contradictions/

Granted, the above sites make for some good reading, but at the center of the debate are the facts that cannot be denied that I have laid out in the history of mankind, especially the history of the Hebrews, that the facts are clear and plain…simply there is no divinity called God.

**Once you get that central fact settled in your head, all issues regarding God melt into just the simple fact of alien visitors of high technological and scientific abilities coming to the underdeveloped Earth and being called God (s).**

One must be careful in criticizing such a document when mankind has rejected in whole or in part numerous writings that have been hotly debated as to their authenticity and their worthiness to be considered inspired writings are given by a God to a scribe. Those writings are as follows.

Contents of " *The Lost Books of the Bible*" [117]

---

- ♦ = attributed to the Apostolic Fathers

- The Protoevangelium
- The Gospel of the Infancy of Jesus Christ
- The Infancy Gospel of Thomas
- The Epistles of Jesus Christ and Abgarus King of Edessa
- The Gospel of Nicodemus (Acts of Pilate)
- The Apostles' Creed (throughout history)
- The Epistle of Paul the Apostle to the Laodiceans
- The Epistles of Paul the Apostle to Seneca, with Seneca's to Paul
- The Acts of Paul and Thecla
- ♦ The Epistles of Clement (The First and Second Epistles of Clement to the Corinthians)
- ♦ The Epistle of Barnabas

---

[117] *Wikipedia s.v.,* "Development of the Christian biblical canon". Document. (Accessed December 20, 2019). https://en.wikipedia.org/wiki/Development_of_the_Christian_b iblical_canon

- ◆ The Epistle of Ignatius to the Ephesians
- ◆ The Epistle of Ignatius to the Magnesians
- ◆ The Epistle of Ignatius to the Trallians
- ◆ The Epistle of Ignatius to the Romans
- ◆ The Epistle of Ignatius to the Philadelphians
- ◆ The Epistle of Ignatius to the Smyrnaeans
- ◆ The Epistle of Ignatius to Polycarp
- ◆ The Shepherd of Hermas (Visions, Commands, and Similitude's)
- Letter of Herod To Pilate the Governor
- Letter of Pilate to Herod
- The Lost Gospel of Peter
- ◆ The Epistle of Polycarp to the Philippians

Contents of *The Forgotten Books of Eden* [116]

---

- The Conflict of Adam and Eve with Satan (The First and Second Book of Adam and Eve)
- The Secrets of Enoch (also known as the Slavonic Enoch or Second Enoch)
- The Psalms of Solomon
- The Odes of Solomon
- The Letter of Aristeas
- The Fourth Book of Maccabees
- The Story of Ahikar
- Testaments of the Twelve Patriarchs

A couple of questions need to be asked at this time. Who or what gave mankind permission to choose what goes into what is claimed to be the "inspired word of God, namely the Bible?"

When this question is asked in a Christian teaching setting i.e., church service, Sunday/Church School, etc., the answer is a quaint "it is given by God as stated in II Timothy, 3:16, (KJV)." The answer is considered final because it is considered that God is the final authority on the matter. There is more to the story than that. If we consider the real and factual origin of God as shown previously in this work, it is proven that God is just the reference for a highly intelligent alien that came to earth and ruled mankind for thousands of years.

The Christian God really confuses the authorship of the Bible because there is no directive in the Bible as to what books are "God-inspired" or not! The two major Christian denominations are, known as Catholicism and nonCatholicism, hold to their separate claims that books in each of their respective Bible are "God-inspired."

The next question is "who gave mankind permission to claim one book as being God-inspired and another book as non-inspired?"

Today, the battle for the answer is not such a hotbed in society because many on both sides of the aisle have drawn back from heated arguments and simply claim that others on the opposite side of the debate are simply misled. In early Biblical history, this was not so!

The canon (authority) of Catholicism regarding Old Testament Biblical books was determined at the Council of Rome in 382 AD. It was that same council that directed Jerome to gather and translate what was considered canonical texts into what came to be known as the Latin Vulgate Bible. As time and conviction moved forward, the Council of Trent in 1546 confirmed the Latin Vulgate Bible as the official Catholic bible because of the changes that Martin Luther made to his German translation, which was on the basis of the original Greek. However, the Church of England and the English Presbyterians made their decision on Biblical content in 1563 in what is called the 39 Articles. Yet, there was the Westminster Confession of Faith in 1647 and the Synod of Jerusalem in 1672 that authored added canons which were greatly accepted throughout the Orthodox Church.[118]

---

[118] Pleune D.R.E., Ronald, (2019.11-13) *The Chariots Flew Then and Still Do Today.* Conneaut Lake, PA: Page Publishing, Inc.

The New Testament canon was a work in progress also through reviews and disputes consisting of 21 books and later to the 27 accepted today. By the time that the First Council of Nicaea, in 325AD, convened, a New Testament list had not been finalized. It wasn't until 367 AD that an Easter letter by the Bishop of Alexandria by the name of Athanasius reflected the same books of the New Testament that is in existence today. The list was accepted by the first council of Rome by Pope Damasus the First in 382 AD and reaffirmed by a second council called the Council of Hippo in 393 AD. It was later accepted by the Council of Carthage in 397 AD and the Council of Carthage in 419 AD. The final book to be accepted was the book of Revelation. Affirmations of the New Testament books were agreed on by the 5th century and ratified by various divisions by 1672. [118]

The above thumbnail sketches are to highlight the rocky and distorted road in the decisions of what would comprise the Old and New Testaments of the Bible. The question that is to be asked here is if God is such a detailed, prayeranswering, human-focused God where he would be concerned that the history of mankind, especially the topic of salvation, then why is determining what is "God given" such a cobbled-up mess? There is a lot more information about the various councils, who was in them and what was said, but in a nutshell, the dissension and turmoil that took place should not have taken place if God had stepped in and set the agenda right in the beginning.

Obviously, this was not the case because there was no God present! In my first book, *"The Chariots Flew Then and Still Do Today,"* I describe the hate and discontent that existed during the Crusades and the Reformation. People were imprisoned and murdered; homes, businesses and churches burned. [119] [120]

---

[119] Gibbons, Katy 2017. *Five of the Most violent Moments of the Reformation*. http://theconversation.com/five-of-the-most-violent-moments-of-the-reformation-71535.

[120] Houghton, S. M. (1980.139-144) Sketches *from Church History*. Edinburgh, London: The Banner of Truth Trust.

This is factual proof that God did not step in and perform a peace miracle, especially when you consider that Protestant and Catholic alike claimed to be "led of God." Major differences existed in doctrine and allegiance to the Pope, which we'll not go into here, since there is a great amount of information about issues and players in Catholicism and the Protestant movement and focus on the main topic of the lack of God in the Creation as well as the affairs of mankind on Earth. [121]

Yes, I can hear your concern over two pivotal questions as follows.

> Q: What about Jesus, the Savior of the world?
>
> A: First of all, nowhere in the Old Testament is the name Jesus mentioned...just the name
>
> Immanuel as in Isaiah 7:14 (KJV). It is also interesting to note that nowhere is it mentioned in Isaiah 7:14 or Isaiah 9:6-7 (KJV) that Immanuel's name would be changed. And, if we look at
>
> Matthew1:22 9 (KJV), we see a false statement because verse 22 states, "And all this was done, that it might be fulfilled which was spoken of the Lord by the prophet, saying...",

Two words are central to the falseness of the Scripture, the first one being the word "all." From the word "all" we are to understand that what was quoted in verse 21 supposedly was quoted by the Lord in Isaiah 7:14 (KJV) or some other Old Testament reference. Isaiah 7:14 says nothing about Immanuel having his name changed to Jesus, and we see nothing about Immanuel "saving his people from their sins," and if we look at the definition of Immanuel, there is not even an inference that he was to "save his people from their sins."

---

[121] Meier, Billy, "Contact 251, p. 1-5," *They Fly*, February 3, 1995. http://www.theyfly.com/.

The second false statement of the Scripture is the statement in Matthew 1:22 (KJV), where it is claimed that it was "spoken of the Lord by the prophet." The problem here is that if the Lord spoke of Immanuel as the one to "save his people from their sins," there are no clear statements of such a promise in the Old Testament by the "Lord." In the matter of interpretation, an inference to something can be confusing at times and lead people to assume "this or that" and stray from the subject at hand or totally mislead people.

## What is the Truth to The Christian Scripture?

The answer is found in Contact Report #251, which I have touched upon earlier in this writing. However, we need to focus on this topic to a greater degree to get a complete understanding of why the Christian Bible is not as reliable as some assume that it is.

The setting for reviewing this topic consists of Billy Meier and one of his teachers from the Pleiades, by the name of Ptaah, discussing various issues. Billy recalls that after approximately 12 billion of years, the people of Enoch split into two groups. Through a series of wars and movements in the universe, one of the groups that had split went to other galaxies, the other group eventually settled on Earth, which up to this point had "retained all knowledge of their earliest origins." These people eventually became known as the Pleiadeans/Plejaren having come from a star cluster beyond the Pleiades.[122]

The group that had split and went to other galaxies lost the knowledge of their heritage, which resulted in their "chroniclers, historians and others to create a different legend about their history." Through time they emigrated to the Sirius Constellation where they were capable of creating new life...bred new human races that were more capable in fighting and manipulating their genes of which one of the consequences was a limitation to their life span to approximately 100 years. Eventually,

---

[122] Ibid. 6-11.

"two large genetically-manipulated peoples fled from the Sirius regions and settled on the opposite side of the Sun, to the Lyra regions and finally to Earth where they "settled in China, Japan and other locations resulting in the formation of various new so-called races."

During this vast history, there were other genetically- manipulated people who emigrated to Mars and Malona/Phaeton. Over time Mars became uninhabitable due to cosmic influences and settled on Earth. Malona/Phaeton was destroyed due to wars by its genetically manipulated residents. The leaders are known as "creator-overlords" from the Sirius Regions, who had originally created the genetically manipulated residents, eventually visited Earth and feared them so much that the "over-lords" destroyed all knowledge of the people's ancestral history. Subsequently, the "over-lords," that is to say those bent on creating the genetically-manipulated people, came back to Earth occasionally to "falsely influence terrestrial individuals with erroneous messages visions and similar things…for they usually only affect the Christian religions and not all terrestrial religions."

**Genetic manipulation of a single DNA is defined as the "original sin," not the disobedience of the man and woman in the Garden of Eden as proclaimed in the Christian Bible.**

**"Yet, in fact, this entire matter is based upon the manipulation of a single DNA gene that can be rectified, if only our geneticists were to finally discover it. This genetic manipulation, a characteristic for all living human beings on Earth by way of its inevitable, hereditary transmission, can be reversed and therefore by doing so, Man can finally escape his evil demeanor, which was imposed upon him by way of genetic manipulation.**[123]

---

[123] Word Press, (2013, document), "Fire from Water: The Way of the True God According to Elijah." Accessed December 28, 2019.
https://jesusweddingthebook.wordpress.com/2013/07/28/fire-from-water-the-way-of-the-true-god/.

So let's place the blame of why mankind on Earth has been led into what is known today as the Christian Religion and why mankind is so selfish, revengeful, hateful, greedy, sly, blameful, inconsiderate, intolerant, dominating, argumentative, selfish, etc., etc., squarely where it needs to be…namely on our ancient ancestors who performed Genetic Manipulation and cooked up religious stories based on a loose outline of historical events as follows.

**"In this manner, the "creator-overlords" were then capable of putting on the airs of terrestrial Man's creators, rising to power and spreading their insane religious doctrines which, however, contained an absolutely novel yet equally false history of humankind's origin, history, and belief. Its purpose was to definitively destroy and lose all data of mankind's true descent in the event that someone else would attempt to secretly glean the information from somewhere."**[124]

## Prayer and Miracles

Those in any Christian religious setting will hear all the Biblical reasons for fostering prayer in their lives from "God is faithful, God never fails, God is longsuffering, God answers in His time, God has a reason," and the jargon continues on and on. What keeps people focusing on Christianity is the wonderment of who, what, when, and how prayer is answered. Mankind has a natural attraction to the "unbelievable" because of the potential outcome as being fascinating and even captivating because of the anticipated answer as being a "WOW" moment in their life.

Prayer is based on the BELIEF that there is a power, such as a deity, that is able to take a situation of reality (i.e., in the matter of weather, health, provisions, safety, and other human needs and wants) and change it to a different and conclusive situation.

Earlier in this work, I have established the fact that there is no God (s), only those that were extraterrestrial who had high abilities in various areas of science and knowledge that dazzled mankind and led mankind to give a deity status to these exceptional aliens.

Today we have the same problem with the facet of prayer… a belief in what someone states occurred that is beyond explanation when requested by mankind.

Floods, fire, and fascinations can be explained by the various avenues of sciences.

For instance, in I Kings, chapter 18 (KJV), there is a contest between the prophets of Baal and Elijah to see who the people will follow. The contest consisted of two altars, one for the prophets of Baal and the other a broken-down altar of the Lord. Additional elements for the fire were water and wood. The deciding factor would be that the fire would ignite and consume the sacrifice. The true occurrence of fire is explained whereby Elijah had an advantage because He repaired an altar that had been burnt by the prophets of Baal. Most likely this alter had been originally made of limestone. (Burnt limestone = quicklime) He probably dressed the oxen offering in the gold of the gods, (sulfur) and poured a mixture of water and naphtha, an ancient form of kerosene, over the whole thing.

For those who are not chemistry savvy, quicklime + sulfur + naphtha = what the ancients call "Automatic Fire." [124]

Other claimed miracles in the Bible such as the parting of the Red Sea, the burning bush, water from a stone, manna from heaven, and

---

[124] Kenwood Travel, (2012, document) "5 Miracles of Moses Explained by Science." Accessed December 28, 2019. HTTPS://www.Kenwoodtravel.co.uk/blog/five-miracles-of-, moses-debunked-by- science/.

*God, The Grandest Illusion*

the ten plagues according to the Book of Exodus in the Bible can be scientifically explained if a person keeps an open mind.[125]

The plagues of Egypt happened as a result of the Destroyer Comet coming unusually close to the Earth. This resulted in huge storms, people and animals died in vast quantities, mountains moved, the depth of the ocean changed and the Santorini volcano on the Mediterranean Sea filled with water and exploded. The toll in human and animal life gave rise to water turning the color of blood which then resulted in the various plagues.[126]

Combined with the above contact Report #5 is the additional information from Wikipedia regarding each of the plagues of Egypt.[127]

Still another great fallacy in "miracles" is in the proper understanding of where and how the waters parted for the Hebrews to cross over the Red Sea… or actually the "Reed Sea."[128]

The way to approach a "miracle" is to understand what it is and what it isn't. A Miracle is an act in an avenue of science such as weather, biology, physiology, etc., in which human understanding is insufficient in comprehending or understanding the wide variations of possibilities within the scope of the present known or unknown laws of science in the cosmos.

---

[125] Billy Meier, "Contact 005, line 58," *They Fly*, February 16, 1975, http://www.theyfly.com/.

[126] Wikipedia s.v. (2019) "The Plagues of Egypt," https://en.wikipedia.org/wiki/Plagues of Egypt.

[127] Lendon, Brad. (2010). "Where did waters part for Moses? Not where you think" CNN blog, September 21, 2010.
http://news.blogs.cnn.com/2010/09/21/where-did-waters-part-for-moses-not-where-you-think/.

[128] Billy Meier, "Contact 251, p. 5-6," *They Fly*, February 3, 1995. http://www.theyfly.com/.

These influences are the direct result of the Spirit of Creation, not of a God, and this force bonds all laws and matter to the Law of Coming and Passing (i.e., that which is born or created and in time passes away in some form or way.

Those are unique explanations in ancient history, but we need to consider prayer and its influence on our present-day lives. Let's look at some examples.

## Blessings

The topic of "blessing (s)" is just as erroneous as the topic of prayer. The study of God in this writing has stated and proven that there is neither a God nor a savior. With that said, there is no blessing from a deity as given in the sample of expressions below.

> I am so blessed by God!
>
> You have a blessed day in the Lord!
>
> God has blessed me so much!
>
> May God bless you in your endeavors!
>
> There are blessings from God in answered prayer!
>
> May God shower you with blessings!
>
> The Lord has blessed me in so many ways!

When the subject of blessings is looked at in the light of them coming from a God other than the Christian God, the blessings are dismissed by Christianity because the train-of-thought is that only the Christian God can place his blessing on people of the Earth because He is held in the position of Head God that exists amongst many other Gods.

We find this out in the King List of the Kings that reigned in Sumeria, where it tells us that they came down from heaven (meaning the cosmos), and each of them reigned for thousands of years. This is recorded in the various clay tablets found in Sumeria, and in particular, the rectangular one that has the "King List" inscribed in it.

The question now comes to mind of "**who has given Christianity the right to state that it is only the Christian God that can or will give blessings to God's people?**"

There are other faiths that believe in a God (s) and yet Christianity will call those followers "heathen." There are people just as blessed in life with a good job, good income, good health, a happy family as well as personal assets who are Hindus, Buddhist, and other eastern faiths as Christians are.

This view is because the same egotistic attitude of mankind created by the genetic manipulation that was performed on mankind as described in *theyfly.com*, Contact Report#70 and#251, dominated the writers of the Biblical Scripture, which led them to claim that there is no other way for mankind to obtain salvation except through Jmmanuel (aka Jesus), Acts 4:12 (KJV). This approach by the Ishwish (meaning alien God and designated with the initials IHWH or JHWH) was planned to keep mankind in servitude and slavery as pointed out in this writing under the heading of Gene Manipulation. The threats continued as they were eventually written down in what is called the Judeo- Christian Scriptures. The statements of God loves…God gives… God guides… God provides…are woven into the Judeo-Christian Scriptures to make it appear that God is a loving and caring God in many ways when in essence, those that do not bow the knee to him will spend eternity in eternal punishment.

What about the "track record" of God of not stepping in to stop wars, hunger, and ruthless rulers in the past! Think of the tragedy of 911 in New York City! If God is what the Judeo-Christian Scriptures say that He is, He certainly knew of the plot and destructive action of those that commandeered the planes into the towers in New York on 9/11/01…yet He did nothing! People in the buildings screamed for God to save them from burning to death or gasping for their last breath as the carnage of building material covered their body…yet no divine intervention took place.

People on the ground stood in awe and wondered as they gasped and expressed the horrific events taking place right before their eyes by stating "God help them" or "Oh my God"…yet no divine intervention took place. People offered prayers to God for mercy and help…yet no divine intervention took place.

Every religious leader in the world should have proclaimed in the next worship gathering of their faith that "there is no God and the demonstration of it is found in the uncaring and non-action that was seen… just like in the Nazi labor camps." These and many other examples of the extermination of human life are a testament to the fact that there is no God or Savior. Instead, people prayed as the destruction of life continued around them. The ugly truth is the following.

No action in a time of need, no grace in a time of anger, and no comfort in a time of hurt!

When will mankind wake up and quit the religious game of blessings from a God that does not respond or care? People will go to their place of worship and pray regarding individual and corporate tragedies. People will fool themselves by thinking that if they pray for themselves or for others, somehow the "icing" of blessing will be spread across the cake of false belief, and we'll all go to our separate homes for their hot Sunday dinner and entertaining ball game on TV.

We hear so many times, especially now when election campaigns are heating up, the familiar ending phrase to their time in front of the microphone or camera "God bless America!" Really? The only reason America is blessed is because of the intestinal fortitude of people coming to America to search for gold in the West, homesteading in the heartland, searching and obtaining employment in the East and South. Many people invented things, expanded commerce, and farmed with the sweat of their brow. Many would say that God blessed them in their endeavors, but the truth of the matter is that God had nothing to do with it...it was by their own initiative to build, plow and provide for their family...because no one else would... including God!

Blessing from God is just a whitewash for the fact that people decided to be pro-active and do something in a country of opportunity. In essence, they took charge of their life.

Taking charge of your life is exactly what the Goblet of the Truth brings to mankind.

To be blessed is to also recognize that the degree of blessing is measured by each person's perspective of themselves in "the satisfaction of what life brings them in the way of meeting their needs and contentment."

Speaking on behalf of God in expressing a blessing is pure erroneous, as well as slanderous to the person that is being addressed when one is telling the other, "may God bless you on your journey," and then the traveling party is killed or severely injured in an accident on their way to their destination. It is here that Christianity backs out of doing a victory dance because a disaster to the other party nullifies a prayer of protection or proclamation of a blessing. The proclamation of blessing, as well as the prayer for safe travel, is not even spoken about in public after the accident since it would prove to be a false reliance on protection and fly in the face of God.

After all, who would follow a God that cannot offer protection on a trip nor a blessing of enjoyment due to being permanently disfigured or crippled for life? Now there will be people who brush this scenario off... until it happens to them. Others would say that it was God's will and continue the rest of their life in not only physical anguish but spiritual anguish because they seek an answer from God; that my friend is not faith, it is a coping mechanism for dealing with the law of 'cause and effect' under the cloak of religion.

Some people use coping strategies of laughing off a matter, throwing something across the room, stating that 'it just wasn't meant to be," or "if I were meant to enjoy the blessing, it would have been different."

What about the person that "T-Boned" your auto and caused one of your passengers to die and you to be physically handicapped the rest of your life? Would you consider it God's will? Would you consider it a blessing from God? Using Education, Rationality, and Logic the answer would be NO!

How should we look at a blessing then? We should look at them in the light of the Laws and Recommendations of the Universe whereby what happens to us is due to 'cause and effect' whether it is for the good or for the bad. Remember, in order for a blessing to occur, there has to be an element of life that creates it or makes it occur. Some examples are as follows, It is a blessing to feel the warm sun after a week of cold and snow. Element: The clouds moved eastward. God did not move the clouds; they moved as part of the weather system.

It is a blessing that our car did not get hit by two other cars. Element: The pavement was dry and allowed the other cars to stop abruptly. God did not make the pavement dry, the wind and the warmth of the sun did.

It is a blessing we didn't get hit by the falling brick. Element: The brick hit a window ledge on the way down and sent it into another direction. God did not place the window ledge in such a way that the falling brick would hit it. It was built that way.

**We find in religions a common thread that once it is pulled will un-do the whole garment. That thread is the thread of "false premise." Wrapped in this mode of guile is the repetitive statement or practice of something that when it is said or done long enough**

**and with convincing speech or actions, it will morph itself into something that people believe is true when in essence it is NOT.**

This, my friend, is the story of religion. We must look life square in the face and see the reality of Truth in the Laws of Science and the Recommendations of how-to live-in peace, freedom, love and harmony as recommended in the Goblet of the Truth. The question is "when will you listen?"

## Answered Prayer or Cause and Effect

In a certain church, the utility obligations were mounting. The congregation met, and the preacher pleaded with the people to give more and more as the offering plate was passed three times before the utility obligations were met.

There was no answer to prayer in this situation or in any situation where money is needed to meet a religious need or even to contribute to someone's personal need. It is simply the fact that the leadership or person in need expressed a certain need that was heard by the members or individuals, and they responded in giving. This was not a matter of God moving the hearts of membership, it was a matter of the membership hearing a need from the pastor and responding so that the church doors would not be locked.

Anytime there is a need expressed by a Christian organization or a person in need, whether it is for money, food, shelter, or some other provision, it is responded by a person's personal desire to help with that call for a provision to be met…not by a God!

The reasoning behind this statement is that any religious group i.e., Hindu, Buddhist, or other Eastern teachings could say the same for people in their group and the meeting of the needs of individual (s) that their God (s) answered their prayer. Yet the Christian will dogmatically state that their God is the only God and not only that but that the

Christian God is the only one that hears their prayers and answers them. This ideology is EXACTLY what the over-lords taught because they wanted to keep people in the "bondage of servitude and slavery" through dogmas of various Christian Faiths that are false.

I have heard many times from the pulpit that God is so awesome and mighty that he doesn't need humans to spread the gospel. Now that's an interesting statement and totally wrong. Think for a moment of these statements.

1) If God was so great, why wait to introduce a savior?

    If any time in history there was a savior needed it certainly was just before the Noah flood because of the universality and magnitude of disobedient and wicked living among mankind!

2) If God was so great, why did he state that mankind should "go and teach all nations" in Matthew 28:19 when it is a foregone conclusion that mankind was in need of the gospel down through the centuries prior to the directive to "go?"

3) If God was so great, then why is it stated in Proverbs 21:1 that "The king's heart is in the hand of the Lord, as the rivers of water: he turneth it whithersoever he will." Yet kings in history that have been a shame to mankind through the power and lack of respect for mankind such as Adolph Hitler, were never dealt with by God, especially since God was supposed to be so mighty and do great things? The carnage of WWII of lost lives through fighting and the murder and extermination of human life serves as a testament that God never existed because he never stepped in and changed the heart of a despot like Adolph Hitler when the verse above states that he (God) can turn the heart of a national leader in whatever way he (God) desires. If this is true, then it would reinforce the fact that God is no better than Adolph Hitler.

Christianity loves to dazzle people with heart-wrenching songs of God's faithfulness, of exquisite sermons that inspire feelings, of so-called answers to prayer that "wow" the crowd…yet fail to see through the smoke and mirrors of inaccurate comprehension of the history of alien influence through genetic manipulation including stories that are completely false regarding the life, teachings, and healing that Jmmanuel (aka Jesus) performed.

How many times have we heard a person of Christian Faith say to someone, "thank you for visiting me, I will pray for your safety as you return home!" And yet, there have been times that an auto accident occurs, and those passengers are hurt or killed. Now, what does the Christian do with that situation? They simply take a "cop-out" and proclaim the following from various Bible passages.

1) It must have been God's will that the situation took place.
2) It was to test your faith.
3) It was to teach you something.
4) The reason will be revealed at some future time.
5) It will make you stronger in your faith.
6) We may never know now or in this lifetime.
7) It will help you in trusting God
8) Trusting God will give you patience and endurance

When we read the multitude of Contact Reports on theyfly.com, we come to realize that they (the Contact Reports) are true because they are factual…more factual and explanatory than any of the Biblical Scripture!

## Prayer In-and-of Itself

Are there any guarantees to an answer?
Does prayer apply to certain matters and not others?

How do we live by faith when praying?
How can we know if a prayer is heard? Being worked on? Or rejected?

Because of our condition of genetic manipulation, the matter of prayer is a heavy tool in the arsenal of control. Genetic manipulation has made us weak in our discretion, fumbling in our search for answers, off-center in looking at life in a logical way, and clouding our rationale reasoning and options in decision making.

The "creator overlords" (those of high scientific and leadership abilities) demanded that they be worshipped as Gods and used clandestine means to get mankind to worship them. In Contact Report #70 their plan is outlined and eventually successful through various influences as shown here. "At this time, **the benefactors elevated themselves to gods and exalted themselves above the terrestrial population, who rapidly became their vassals and believers**. Truthfully, in doing so, the benefactors very soon became the antithesis of benefactors. On the one hand, they hoped to make the genetically-manipulated people their subjects and that, on the other, **many cults, religions, fratricide, family feuds and wars would be launched through this worship of gods**, whereby the terrestrials, the genetically-manipulated people, would decimate and exterminate themselves."[129]

Let's stop the merry-go-round of confusion and look back at our society today. We have constant wars, crime of all depths, greed for power, and self at all levels, including private and public sectors. When are we going to admit that all religion is a farce and that we need to learn selfresponsibility, accountability, social justice, and recognition of our Ur ancestry regarding gene manipulation and the false teachings of our ancestors from the cosmos?

---

[129] Billy Meier, "Contact 32, line 324-329," *They Fly*, September 8, 1975, http://www.theyfly.com/.

We have completely forgotten our ancestral roots from the Cosmos, our Ur, Ur, and Ur "ad infinitum" ancestry and now have come to regretfully rely on Biblical writings that are:

1) Incomplete in the history of mankind
2) Inaccurate in Scriptural dating
3) Incomplete in what is Scriptural truth and what is not
4) Irresponsible in leaving humans to determine what writings should be in a Bible
5) Inconsistent in referencing a verse to an incident, i.e., Isaiah 7:14 to Matthew 1:21-23

It bears repeating regarding the substance of religion from Semjase, one of the main teachers from the planet Erra that was told to Billy Meier about the founding and teachings of religion as follows.[130] "So when the terrestrial religions are spoken of negatively through Semjase, what is being addressed were and are the distortions and lies which are built into the religions, partly in a consciously deceitful way." (This is in reference to the gene manipulation by extraterrestrials held as Gods discussed previously). "By this however are also addressed those sheer human, infamous concoctions, which you have commonly known as heresies and dogmas; sheer infamous concoctions by irresponsible or mistaken Earth humans, which through these heresies they have started, are able to beat your entire humanity into consciousness-based poverty and servitude. The terrestrial religions are religions only in name because in reality, they are not such, but only cultic degenerations in a very evil sense. Religions in this form are always false and deadly. In reality, they should not be called religions but cults. In your case, we call them cultic religions because real religion-related facts are interspersed with cultic dogmas and heresies and adulterated."

---

[130] Billy Meier, (2001, document), "Questions to Billy Meier," http://www.theyfly.com/gaia/answers.html

*Dr. Ron Pleune*

## Prayer and Physical Healing

One of the most powerful fallacies of Christianity regarding miracles is physical healing. I have told the story many times of the young man in the hospital that was deathly ill. He had six friends composed of a Baptist, Christian Reformed, Jew, Muslim, Seventh Day Adventist, and Catholic. The disease was announced as terminal, and the man's friends said they would pray for his recovery in earnest. A few days after the announcement of the terminal illness, the young man passed away. His friends came to the hospital and found the bed empty and with clean linen. They asked at the Nurse station where the young man had been taken, and the response was that he had passed away in the night.

The question here is, "with all the prayer that was made on behalf of the young man, why weren't the prayers of his friends answered?"

Going back to the example of the young man who was ill in the hospital and looking at it from the standpoint that the man was healed, the next question is "whose deity/God would receive the credit for healing?" And if the man had died, could the finger of faithlessness be pointed at any or all of the man's friends for lack of faith? Or was it a lack of action by their God?

In reviewing the definition of God earlier in this writing, we find that God is nothing more than a human of advanced technological and scientific knowledge and expertise. His power in the matters of men is limited to the laws of the universe…essentially what he can and cannot produce or make happen with the wisdom of material and scientific invention. So, anything beyond his ability will rest with the expression "it was not God's will" or be accepted as the "Law of Cause and Effect."

Man has been led into the delusion of the power of prayer through written and verbal pronouncements from the Christian Bible. Prayer is called "faith-gambling" because if you win, you tell every one of your winnings which equates to answered prayer. Yet if you don't win, you walk away hurt and sad, especially if you lay in your hospital bed with a terminal disease, and all the prayers and laying- on of hands with oil does nothing for you.

So, what is the correct approach to prayer, and how should it be applied today?

The frustration in mankind can be seen in the excuses and cover-ups that come out of the mouth of people because they do not have a clear understanding of prayer. Mankind for the most part likes a security blanket which is called prayer because it relates mankind to a "force" which in Christianity is to a God that does not exist nor able to perform miracles. It is also used as a social "tag" that when you speak of praying for someone, it identifies you as being a part of so-called God's family as well as identifying yourself as believing in something that is "magical."

The falsehood of prayer comes when nothing results from your prayer or something does happen that is completely opposite from what you prayed for! When a tornado goes down the opposite side of the street that you live on and you come out of your home afterwards and see the destruction, you would probably say "thank God my family and I were spared and we are all alive!" Yet a few houses down and across the street there was a family that was not so fortunate, and all family members perished. You cannot thank God for anything because the weather "is what it is" and will act according to the laws of science (nature) in how it forms, where it goes and how intense it will be. This, my friend is the "reality" of life and of facing "cause and effect" in all that surrounds us including the actions that we take or do not take.

Christian believers are committing an undeniable mistake in thinking that they are blessed beyond measure by prayer when in fact thousands of people of different faiths around the world perish due to various diseases and disasters. Why them? Because they are no different than the Christian believers, they all face fate through "cause and effect" which is the result of the genetic mutations that cause mankind to be vindictive in various ways and unable to cope with the negative events of life.

Billy Meier has a question and answer section on http://www.theyfly.com/gaia/answers.html in which a person by the name of Norm asked Billy if a spinal cord injury and paralysis that came about when run over by a car could be cured by meditation (i.e. prayer). Billy's answer was that "meditation cannot be used for such physical healing." [131]

The question that comes up now is "why the technicality?" First of all, there is no God to pray to which brings up the next question, "who do I pray to?" At this point of writing, I must admit to the reader that what Billy explains next is going to be a tough pill to swallow, but once you work it out in your understanding through slow and careful reading, you will grasp the truth and the simplicity of it.

Billy writes the following (revised for flow of thought from German to English).

1. The first possibility is that you <u>pray simply to the allembracing, genderless and personality-less Creation.</u> And when you do that, then you speak with it through your own self in your working creation-given spirit-form, i.e., your spirit (within you) enlivening you, which enlivens through its energy in your consciousness. Thereby you speak or pray indirectly with your consciousness, i.e., carry a conversation in this manner. 2. The second is that you, with a prayer, directly address your spirit-form (the spirit within you), whereby you then also in an indirect way communicate with your own consciousness.[132]

Prayer, as also in the form of meditation, through your spirit-form (spirit) is energy of the Creation which you can transmit through your

---

[131] Billy Meier, (2010, 1-2), "Reader Question: To whom should I address my Prayers," *http://www.figu.org/ch/verein/periodika/bulletin/2010/nr-71/leserfrage.*

[132] Billy Meier, (2010, 3), "Reader Question: To whom should I address my Prayers," *http://www.figu.org/ch/verein/periodika/bulletin/2010/nr-71/leserfrage.*

consciousness. Therefore, it can also travel from the consciousness of one person to the consciousness of another person…not to the healing of flesh and bone. When you pray in tandem with the energy of your spirit, you can master your own destiny as Billy Meier describes here, as it is revised for the flow of thought from German to English. When you address your spirit within you, then you speak automatically to your consciousness, which itself very quickly gets accustomed consequently <u>you influence your will</u> and can achieve what you want. Naturally, you can at your own discretion also freely use conversation prayers, in which you include those things which occupy you and which you want to achieve.

You can completely shape this after your own will; therefore, you can be sure that it really functions. When you feel yourself powerfully for it, then you can also use a conversational-prayer-based approach directly to your consciousness and communicate with it. This means that you simply express your thoughts and feelings clearly, precisely, and rationally so that you determine you own will and work toward those things that you strive for, come about, and are fulfilled. This is also applicable when you have to master grief because in the course of this you must determine how the grief management for yourself has to be resolved. When you have these types of personal needs, communicate rationally with your consciousness (as in selftalk), then everything regulates itself in accordance with that, as you strive for and fulfill it.[133]

The question that comes to mind is "what about the healing that Jmmanuel (aka Jesus) supposedly did?" The Talmud of Jmmanuel answers that question quite emphatically as well as the previous question to Billy Meier of the person who had a spinal cord injury. Simply put, prayer will not heal a physical condition, whether by disease or physical accident.

The authenticity of the Talmud of Jmmanuel, as covered in chapter 2 of this work, speaks of several situations where physical and mental healing took place, **but not by the element of prayer.** Those examples are as follows.

---

[133] Billy Meier, (2016, 142), *Talmud of Jmmanuel*, Landesgruppe, Canada.

Dr. Ron Pleune

In chapter 8, we read about the healing of the leper. It is important to understand that the disease of leprosy must be specially treated through medical means. What the Bible fails to explain is that the leper had resolved himself to the fact that he had leprosy, but the more impending problem was that the leper had a difficult time coping with the pain and discomfort of leprosy.

In the Talmud of Jmmanuel, the record tells us that Jmmanuel stretched out his hand and touched him, a sign of sympathy and identifying the fact that they were both human and susceptible to pain and suffering. Then, Jmmanuel "spoke long and deeply (suggestively) to him."[134] This action is actually a counseling session that lasted for a period of time which is exactly what Isaiah 9:6 said Jmmanuel would be, "Counselor."

Billy Meier explains that there are charlatans and delusional believers who actually believe they have spiritual healing powers and help from a deity. This can be seen on TV with the "healing services" or addendum to a Christian Biblical message where a certain portion of time is set aside for the "laying on of hands" and "anointing of oil" for the healing of a physical illness or accident. There are those that have sprung to a healthy situation at the time of a "healing service" due to overpowering inner energy (called expectation) that has brought a temporary healing, or the combination of mental coping and the body chemicals that have come together to bring about a restoration of a body function and mental relief.[135]

Another example was of the servant of the centurion who was incapacitated with gout which was affecting the servant's suffering in his mind. Jmmanuel consented to see the servant, at which time he gave the servant an herbal potion that calmed him.[136] Once again, life

---

[134] Ibid, (150-152).

[135] Ibid, (144-148).

[136] Whiteman, Honor, (2017, document), "The Lazarus Phenomenon: When the 'dead' come back to life," accessed 12/30/19. https://www.medicalnewstoday.com/articles/317645.php.

will bring illnesses that will drive us out of our senses by making us cry or possibly respond in physical anger. We need to avail ourselves to prescription or herbal treatments to cope with the situation.

Various examples of prayer are as follows.

Use your own thoughts and feelings with inward speaking or speaking outward (out loud).

Example toward **others**- *physical injuries/pain*: Spirit within me, give your power to John to relieve the pain and anguish he experiences from the injuries he sustained in his fall from the ladder.

Example toward **others**- *social loss/pain of endurance/worry*: Spirit within me, give your power in comforting John as he is coping with the loss of his mother.

Example for **personal**- *physical pain:* Spirit within me, give your power of relief from pain. Help me to cope with the discomfort of my injury so that I can function more effectively including the healing process and ultimate recovery.

Example of **personal** social loss/pain of endurance/worry: nervousness, anxiety, etc. Spirit within me, give your power in comforting me as I cope with the loss of my mother.

Example for **personal** *accomplishing of something*: Spirit within me, give me wisdom and strength to accomplish this task. Help me to focus on it and to work with others with integrity, honesty and fairness.

Example for **personal** *failure*: Spirit within me, I have failed in being what I should have been today; I acknowledge my error (s) and ask for your guidance in my thought (s).

When you free yourself through the truth about the ancient civilizations and the alien influence it has had on who we are and why we respond the way that we do because of genetic manipulation and false teachings of what came to be the Christian faith and doctrine which in turn influenced mankind's belief in prayer and many other dogmas, you begin to see the larger picture and leave the Christian dogmas of "you must believe and do" aside. You will begin to see the misguided Christian history and forge the reality of determining your own life…not a deity.

## Prayer and Death

We can gain more knowledge about the falseness of prayer through the example of a person passing away and was claimed to have been brought "back to life through prayer." Mankind has once again been led into error through the expectation of something great happening, especially those that are prone to the notion that prayer can accomplish or bring about a wished-for event.

An illustration of something that happened to me may be of some benefit. A few years ago, I was turkey hunting, and a big "Tom" turkey walked within range along with many hen turkeys. After ensuring that the hens were not going to be hit with the BB's, I downed the Tom with one shot. The turkey fluttered on the ground and then lay motionless. After several minutes, I got up from my seat and walked over to the turkey; it was motionless. The morning was cold, and I had cloth gloves on my hands which turned out to be beneficial to the situation. I took hold of the feet and lifted it up…then to my surprise, the turkey came back alive and fluttered its wings which made it twirl like an upside-down helicopter. As it did, its feet became caught in my gloves and began to tear them along with my hand. I immediately dropped the turkey and gloves on the ground. What I had assumed to be dead was not really dead because the blood in the turkey rushed oxygen to its brain, and the turkey appeared to "come back alive."

What do we learn from this? The turkey was not dead; it gave the appearance that it was dead, but the process of life (oxygen, blood, electrical impulses, etc.) had not ceased its function. This is no different than a person who seemingly has passed away.

A number of examples have been given in "Medical News Today" regarding the issue of death and when the dead come back.[137] They are as follows.

In 2001, a 66-year-old man had a cardiac arrest, resuscitation efforts were conducted for 17 minutes including CPR, defibrillation and medication. He was pronounced dead, yet **10 minutes later,** a pulse was detected.... he was alive!

In 2014, a 78-year-old man was declared dead after a hospice nurse noted he had no pulse. The **next day** he woke up, bagged, and in the morgue!

In 2007, a report was made by Vedamurhy Adhiyaman that approximately 82% of Lazarus syndrome cases ROSC (return of spontaneous circulation) occurred within 10 minutes of CPR being stopped.

In 2014, an 80-year-old woman was **frozen alive** in a hospital morgue after being incorrectly pronounced dead.

In 2014, a woman was **pronounced brain dead** yet awoke shortly after being taken to the operating room for organ harvesting.

In 2013, a woman gave birth to a baby on a sidewalk in the frigid cold temperature. Doctors were unable to detect a pulse and consequently the baby was pronounced dead...**yet two hours later** the baby began moving! Dr. Michael Klein of the U. of British Columbia in Canada stated that "though circulation would have stopped, the neurological condition of the child could be protected by the cold."

In death, there are actually two types of death: clinical death and biological death. **Clinical death** is defined as the absence of a pulse,

---

[137] Ritchie, George G. (1978), *Return from Tomorrow*. Waco, Texas: Chosen Books.

heartbeat, and breathing, while **biological** death is defined as the absence of brain activity.

In 1943, a man in basic training at Camp Barkeley, Texas, by the name of George Ritchie died of a double-lobar pneumonia. He was dead for nine minutes before returning back to life.[138]

Billy Meier explains the two types of death through an article by Jacob Simits whereby **Clinical** Death occurs when all vital functions are reduced to an absolute minimum, but the brain still has some electrical activity. **Brain** Death is defined as being an irreversible loss of all functions of the brain in which there is no electrical activity in the brain and no blood flow to the brain. In this situation the bodily functions are maintained by machines i.e. breathing, blood flow, intravenous feeding, etc. [139]

An unusual incident was of a woman who was put on life support and "supposedly" dead for 17 hours because no pulse was detected. Prayers were offered up but no response. Soon after being taken off life support, the lady began moving her limbs when "suddenly her heart restarted according to the nurse. The doctor stated that surviving three long periods (of attempted resuscitation) without a heart rate is less than 10 percent.[140]

What should be pointed out here is that prayer was not a factor in igniting the continuation of life; it is simply the coordination of bodily functions in tandem with the electrical brain activity.

---

[138] Billy Meier, (2004, document), "Death, Afterlife and Rebirth, by Jacob Simits," http://www.futureofmankind.co.uk/Billy Meier/Death, Afterlife and Rebirth.

[139] Elsworth, (Catherine, 2008, document), "Woman Comes Back to Life after Being Dead for 17 Hours" accessed 12/30/19. https://www.telegraph.co.uk/news/newstopics/howabout

[140] Billy Meier, (2012, document), "Life, Death and Rebirth," http://www.meiersaken.info/Reinkarnation.html

*God, The Grandest Illusion*

## Out-of-body Experiences

This topic brings up the subject of out-of-body experiences where a person is observed as going through the throngs of death or seemly has passed on. Billy Meier explains this in the following terms. "The said human beings were in truth not dead, but rather only seen to be clinically dead, which means that no more verifiable heart and brain activity exists. This, however is as said; only a clinical death, with which, however, the spirit-form has not yet left the body, but rather still continues to live in this. Also, therefore the overall consciousness moreover still lives in the physical body, even if the life functions of each form appear to be extinguished. Since now the overall consciousness and the spirit-form still live in the body, which as the case may be can still last seconds, minutes or hours and under certain circumstances even years and decades, as e.g., during shock freezing for surviving, etc., also then the consciousness still works. However, this occurs only in death throes form, which is why also no more brain activity can be ascertained, nevertheless it actually occurs. During this process pictures tread down into appearance, which correspond to the thought and the fantasy of the concerned human beings, who become, however also dominated by

that/2032591/Woman-comes-back-to-life-after-being- dead-for-17-hours.html.

the earth-human overall-collective. And in this low death throes state, it often becomes possible for the concerned human beings, to send out their consciousness, whereby they suddenly from the outside can see themselves floating over themselves, etc. Light and darkness and human loved ones very often play an important role, as, e.g., that the death-throes of light forms etc. through dark channels etc. to be led into the light, from where they do not again want to return, etc." [142]

I had a personal friend by the name of Joe that went through such an experience while being operated on for a repeated hernia situation.

117

When he awoke in the recovery area, the doctor came in and said that he had something to tell Joe. Joe said that he already knew what the doctor was going to say and began telling the doctor that he had "died" twice on the operating table, and they revived him using a defibrillator. The doctor confirmed what Joe had said, but then Joe went on to say how each of those two times he felt his "presence or existence" lift out of his body and floating near the ceiling where he heard and saw all that was going on between those in the room.

The important thing to understand here is that Joe was not dead; only his heart had stopped beating. He was still clinically alive!

Billy explains that the "overall consciousness and the spiritform still live in the body." As Billy explains, this can last for "seconds, minutes or hours and under certain[141] for "seconds, minutes or hours and under certain circumstances even years and decades, as e.g. during shock freezing for surviving, etc., also then the consciousness still works. However, **this occurs only in death throes form**, which is why also no more brain activity can be ascertained, nevertheless it actually occurs." The concept and process of this out-of-body experience is mysterious to say the least, but it is definable and can be understood through Billy Meier's explanation in his write-up of "Life, Death, and Rebirth." [142]

## Beyond the Grave- The Spirit of Each Individual

Earlier in this work, the question was asked; what keeps people holding onto a religion such as Christianity?

---

[141] Billy Meier, (© **FIGU 1996-2020, document**), "**Interview: Spiritual Teaching with Billy Eduard Albert Meier,**" accessed 1/3/20. https://creationaltruth.org/FIGU/Spiritual-Teaching/The- Spiritual-Teaching/Interview-Spiritual-Teaching.

[142] Billy Meier, *Goblet of the Truth*. (Canada: FIGU-Landsgruppe Canada, 2015, 383&385, verse 16).

One of the answers, and a very important one is that there is fear in death. People, by far and wide, do not like the idea of their spirit, and in some beliefs the soul, will go nowhere or be damned to a place of torment. Others believe that their soul will go to a Heaven based on either their good works on Earth or their being born again through a belief in Jesus Christ. As shown previously in this work, there is no Heaven or Hell, which begs the question of where the Spirit within mankind goes after death?

In order to understand the answer to this question, we need to identify where the Spirit of a person resides. In the Christian faith, the Spirit is the motivator and lives within the individual; the Soul is a persona of the human, which is often referred to as a ghost.

In the Teaching of the Truth, there is no soul, just a Spirit aka Spirit-form (energy) that resides in the region of the superior Colliculus until the human passes away. [143] The Spirit is immortal and escapes the human body at the human's death and goes into its realm of the "other world" of the overall consciousness block (which can be likened to a blank CD or memory stick). It liberates the consciousness-block and the personality from everything that was still not processed during the actual life by processing such. After that, the consciousness, or rather, the entire consciousness-block with the personality unique to it becomes dissolved into pure, neutral spirit-energy, from which, by means of the overall consciousness-block, a new consciousness, or rather, a completely new consciousnessblock becomes created, in which an absolutely new personality is integrated, which is no longer identical to the old, deceased one. This new consciousness-block and new personality then become incarnated, or born, when the spirit-form reincarnates in a new human.[144]

---

[143] Billy Meier, (2016, 362), *Talmud of Jmmanuel*, Landesgruppe, Canada.

[144] Jacob Smits, (2004 Document), *Death, Afterlife and Rebirth*, http://www.futureofmankind.co.uk/Billy Meier/Death, Afterlife and Rebirth.

The term "block" above does not mean an action to stop something from coming through, it is a designation of space that contains the consciousness, sub-consciousness and the new personality. It can be likened to a blank CD or memory stick ready for recording life's experiences.

The Afterlife is the time that the Spirit spends in a Spiritual reality. For the Earth human, this is normally 1.52 times his/her physical life, which means that when a person dies at age 75, the Spirit will spend 114 years in the afterlife. An example of this is when Jane Doe is born in the year 1925 and died in the year 2000, her Spirit will reincarnate in the year 2114.[145]

In its time, the Spirit will be animated in a new person 21 days after conception (the time when the heart will begin to beat) and be considered as a "living human," [146] [147] [148]

## Jmmanuel (Immanuel/Emmanuel) and Salvation

Biblical scribes have always created their own "mysterious" scenarios about Biblical events. As already shown, many of those scenarios had been taught by the over-lords of various alien groups to confuse mankind due to genetic-manipulation and the need of the over-lords (those of high scientific knowledge and known to Earth humans as God/Gods) to dominate and control their subjects as stated here.

---

[145] Billy Meier, "Contact 007, line 196," *They Fly*, February 25, 1975, http://www.theyfly.com/.

[146] Billy Meier, (2001, Document), *Billy Answers Questions,* http://www.theyfly.com/gaia/answers.html.

[147] 149-Billy Meier, "Contact 260, line 74," *They Fly*, February 3, 1998, http://www.theyfly.com/.

[148] Billy Meier, "Contact 251, p. 5-7," *They Fly*, February 3, 1995. http://www.theyfly.com/.

"The genetically-manipulated people have since established themselves on Earth to the degree where they simultaneously became this planet's rulers and its destroyers, because most of them remained overly entangled in the effects of the manipulated genes of fighting, viciousness, barbarism, bloodthirstiness, greediness, addiction, emotionalism, inhumanities, to name but a few. These characteristics have been an evil legacy for mankind from early times, and they also may actually be called **the "original sin".** Information regarding the "original sin" was erroneously handed down by Christian religions as the fable of **Adam, Eve and the devilish snake in the Garden of Eden.** This "**original sin**", however, the genetic manipulation, repeatedly let the obsession for fighting and evil to surface from time immemorial- almost becoming Evil itself." [149]

In Christianity, the purpose of the crucifixion is that there had to be a blood sacrifice for the sins of mankind, of which it is written that Emmanuel, wrongly called Jesus, was to be "that" sacrifice. There are a number of problems with this matter which will be addressed below.

First of all, as pointed out above, the question of "sin" is defined as the act of genetic manipulation on mankind, which was covered earlier in this work.

Secondly, the writing of Isaiah was in Hebrew, yet the so-called gospel of Matthew was written in Greek. Obviously, there was a mistranslation between the two languages or a misunderstanding of the "angel of the Lord" as to the child's name in Matt. 1:20 (KJV).

Thirdly, none of the original gospels exist today, which you would think that if God was so almighty and powerful He would ensure correct data to be preserved.

Fourth, the name "Jesus" was never stated or even inferred to in Isaiah 7:14 nor in Isaiah 9:6-7. Billy Meier explains that Jmmanuel was not named "Jesus' or 'Yeshua' (Hebrew for 'Yahweh is the salvation') at his

---

[149] Billy Meier, (2016, CXXVIII), *Talmud of Jmmanuel*, Landesgruppe, Canada.

birth by his mother or foster father but rather 'Jmmanuel', completely in accordance with Isaiah's prediction, which was well known to the two by the celestial son, Gabriel. The name 'Jesus Christ' is made up, accordingly, from the Greek form of the Jewish proper name 'Yeshua' and the epithet 'Christ'.[150] A more detailed explanation is given by James W. Deardorff titled "Was His Name Originally Jesus, or Immanuel? [151]

Fifth, (Biblical references are all KJV) the reference in Matthew 1:23 to Isaiah 7:14 as being a "sign" from the Lord himself" is a direct violation of Isaiah 7:14 that indeed the child should be called Immanuel.

Sixth, the term "God with us" needs to be understood in the context of ancient alien influence on mankind as being "Gods." Yet if we rightly read and understand the Talmud of Jmmanuel we read that Jmmanuel (the Jesus referred to in Matthew 1:21 (KJV) is a mere man that has the scientific knowledge to work with nature in using the natural herbs and plant compounds to heal various illnesses and injuries.

Seventh, the Biblical Scripture (Biblical references are all KJV) contradicts itself when in Isaiah 7:15-16 it states that the child (referring to Immanuel) "shall know to refuse the evil, and choose the good" which is in direct opposition to other portions of Scripture that state that Immanuel could not commit sin nor any sinful communication come out of his mouth, I Peter 2:22, 2 Corinthians 5:21. Hebrews 4:15, I John 3:5, I Peter 1:18-19. As a young child he would partake of the milk (referring to rudimentary learning experiences that aid in growth), and honey (which refers to the more nourishing experiences in fortifying, regulating, cleansing, and healing the whole body).

---

[150] James Deardorff, (1998, document), Was His Name Originally Jesus, or Immanuel? https://www.scribd.com/document/192699347/2012- James-W-Deardorff-Was-His-Name-Originally-Jesus-Or- Immanuel.

[151] Billy Meier, "Contact 006, lines 28-32" *They Fly*, February 23, 1975. http://www.theyfly.com/.

## Repentance and Eternal Life

As previously mentioned, the term "sin" is a specific term to lead man into servitude and enslavement to a nonexistent God. This in turn, results in a lack of selfdevelopment and self-accountability.

The correct terminology and description are embodied in the term "error." Billy Meier and one of his main friends and instructors by the name of Semjase, discuss this briefly as it relates to "sin." She defines "sin" as a "self-inflicted error and that it must be made good again." Billy Meier goes on to say that "one encounters no guilt if he commits errors in life, for which he can make amends in the way that he recognizes the error, or whatever one wants to call it, no longer commits it, and takes it in as knowledge, from which then, certain wisdom must result?" Semjase responds that Billy has expressed the "deepest core of the truth." [152]

To clarify, "sin" is a self-inflicted error that must be reconciled, or as Semjase puts it "must be made good again." If you have transgressed someone in word or deed, the relationship must be put a-right again as if nothing had happened in the first place. This means communicating with the other person the sorrow you feel for having harmed them physically and/or mentally so that there is a friendly relationship that is put back in place…which may take some time.

Not only that, but in reality a person who had committed an "error" needs to set the offense towards another person (s) in a proper perspective in their own heart because the offender has not only committed an "error" against another or others, but has also committed an "error" against themselves due to the fact that they have transgressed their own integrity of being a person of love, honor and truth.

How is this put in motion? Through the honest and sorrowful acceptance of the offending person's responsibility of acknowledging

---

[152] Billy Meier, *Goblet of the Truth*. (Canada: FIGU-Landsgruppe Canada, 2015, 515).

they have hurt another human through their words or actions. This involves the offending person praying to their Spirit and with 1) the said <u>acknowledgment</u> of harm that was done, and 2) requesting that the <u>Spirit within to help</u> them in changing their attitude and actions to a positive response by learning to listen, learning to be sympathetic, learning not to jump to conclusions, learning to be patient, learning to take in all facts and facets and practicing self-control through selftherapy (self-talk) and/or the help from another trusted individual to remind them of their need for restraint, calm, and consideration through the mode of ERL, Education, Rationality and Logic.[153]

There is no need for a savior to confess your errors to; confess them to the offended person (s). There is no need for fear of punishment since punishment is instantly meted at the time of the offense due to your conscience realizing that you have harmed a person (s) and that you need to set the matter right. Until such time comes, you will endure (receive in your conscience) the punishment of knowing you have harmed someone who you really need to acknowledge to them that you were in "error" and ask them to forgive you. If at this time they fail to respond positively to your honest actions, then let the matter go… they will have to live with their failure to acknowledge your contrite regret and the matter will rest with their conscience as an unfulfilled matter on their part.[154]

A further word of explanation concerns punishment that is external. Though you have made peace between you and the other person, there still may be consequences lawfully.

Though this course may be hard to bear after full confession and resulting forgiveness by others and between you and your Spirit, sentencing through lawful procedure most likely will pursue due to

---

[153] Billy Meier, *Goblet of the Truth*. (Canada: FIGU-Landsgruppe Canada, 2015, 503).

[154] Billy Meier, *Goblet of the Truth*. (Canada: FIGU-Landsgruppe Canada, 2015, 171& 175).

the fact that a crime against civil law has taken place and will serve as a deterrent towards others in the future.[155]

As one studies the Laws and Recommendations through the Goblet of the Truth, the term "throwback" is also used to describe "errors." This term gets at the heart of the negative results of an "error" which is acknowledging that a "throwback" is an action that puts you in a state of negative position that actually throws you back from moving forward in a positive motion with fellow mankind. The opposite of "throwback" is "move forward" which takes the attitude of setting a situation in a positive motion as previously discussed.

Another term, or synonym, for "errors" or "throwbacks" is the word "misdeeds." None of these words either individually or collectively, are intended to soften the negative fallout of a situation between a person and person (s), they simply mean the same thing with the same impact as to a lack of responsibility and consideration for another human being. [156]

Being human has made it hard at times to move forward in a positive path with others…we all know that! Some great counsel in the Goblet of the Truth states that when these "error" or "falls in life" occur, we need to accept that they are 1) unavoidable, they will happen some time or another, and maybe when we least expect it; 2) we need to learn from the experience, not bury ourselves in remorse, selfrevenge and possibly a life style of reclusiveness. [157] The key is to STOP and ask yourself (and being honest with yourself) what can I learn from this situation? What was my part in it? How can I approach a similar situation in a different and more respectful way in the future? The last step is learning to rise above the matter so that you, as well as others, can move forward in

---

[155] Billy Meier, *Goblet of the Truth*. (Canada: FIGU-Landsgruppe Canada, 2015, 583).

[156] Billy Meier, *Goblet of the Truth*. (Canada: FIGU-Landsgruppe Canada, 2015, 181).

[157] Billy Meier, *Goblet of the Truth*. (Canada: FIGU-Landsgruppe Canada, 2015, 169, 283).

life while feelings go through a period of calming down, re-assessing matters, and setting a course of peace and harmony. [158]

In regards to the outcome of errors/sin/throwbacks/misdeeds, mankind has been led to believe in a Heaven and Hell, or in other words, a reward or punishment. We are taught that for obedience we receive a reward; for disobedience a punishment.

In Christianity especially, there are a couple of schools of thought on this topic. The first one is that once you are drawn by God's calling to receive Jesus as your savior, you are guaranteed the destination of Heaven; this is known as "once saved, always saved." The other choice or school of thought is that a person has a free will of whether they want to accept the invitation to salvation and eternal life. There are various arguments for these two points of view in which each uses Biblical Scripture. [159]

The question of eternal security has always been a bone of contention because there are a great number of splinter questions that arise, such as; if a child is born and then dies at one year of age, do they have the assurance of eternal life? Or, what about those that are mentally handicapped and do not have the ability to fathom out what to choose? What about a person that is coerced or talked-into a decision, would it stand up to a truly personal decision for salvation? As I have stated, many other splinter questions have arisen, and they lead to confusion as well as disharmony amongst religious communities. This is typical of the Christian faith and Scriptures, which results in a lot of arguing that drives people to hatred and down-talking of other denominations. Still, others will try to sugarcoat the matter and state that there is more that unites them than what divides them…. yet the disharmony

---

[158] Robinson, Jerry (Document), *The Doctrine of Eternal Security: Differing Views,* Accessed 1/12/20, https://truerichesradio.com/the-doctrine- of-eternal-security-differing-views/.

[159] Billy Meier, *Goblet of the Truth.* (Canada: FIGU-Landsgruppe Canada, 2015, 207, 57, 499, 171, 455).

*God, The Grandest Illusion*

still continues because, for the most part, we humankind like to have definitive answers that we feel comfortable and can rely on.

Where does it end? It begins and ends with the REAL TRUTH as described in the Contact Notes for real human beings that have been to the corners of the Universe and testify that there is no heaven and no hell. Earlier in this work there was an entire page of references to the fact that there is no such place as hell. The following are some references from the Goblet of the Truth to the fact that there is no Heaven. [160]

Pg. Ch. Vs.

|  | Vs | Pg | Ch |
|---|---|---|---|
| Heaven- a state of inner being made by yourself | 207 | 6 | 71 |
| Heaven- is false and just an invention by those in delusion which puts people in bondage of thoughts | 57 | 2 | 326 |
| Heaven- is not a place but rather condition in yourselves | 499 | 28 | 49 |
| Heaven- false teachings and fundamentally wrong | 499 | 28 | 49 |
| Heaven- is within you | 171 | 5 | 32 |
| Heaven- is within you | 455 | 25 | 203 |

Now I ask you, if you needed something to be verified, such as the building of a sporting goods store several miles away that you've wanted to come to your area but you have not seen nor heard of the building progress, would you believe a trustworthy person's verification so that you could plan on visiting it when it opens up? Of course!

The same is true of what the Plejaren have verified and spoken to Billy Meier about what goes on in our Universe. Therefore, Billy relied on the

---

[160] Billy Meier, "Contact 252, lines 76-80" *They Fly*, February 14, 1995. http://www.theyfly.com/.

information that was communicated to him and recorded in documents such as the Contact Reports and many in pictures of Plejaren spaceships.

Now I must confess that I doubted the reality alien life, especially the Plejaren, until my wife and I began using light signaling in August of 2016, to contact UFO. Within the first 30 days of signaling we had several flyovers of UFO approximately 300-400 feet above us. And within those first 30 days we had a Plejaren ship come down and hover a few feet off the ground, all lit up in two 15 second intervals just 300 feet from our car. The ship was exactly the same as Semjase's ship! Yes, they are still around, Contact Report #252 tell us that they still monitor our Earth's activities through observation flights both manned and unmanned.[161]

## The Gospels

The Talmud of Jmmanuel covers in essence what was known as the Gospel of Matthew. The question now comes to the forefront of why there is such a difference between the two. In this work it was pointed out that the Talmud of Jmmanuel was written by Judas Ischkerioth and it begs the question now of why didn't Mark and Luke reflect the same tone and harmony of information as the Talmud of Jmmanuel which replaced the Gospel of Matthew?

Just as in solving a crime, the question is asked, "were there any witnesses?"

**Judas Ischkerioth**, the writer of the Talmud of Jmmanuel, was present during the life of Jmmanuel and wrote Jmmanuel's life down.

**Mark** was not on scene to be an eyewitness to the events of Jesus (Jmmanuel's life). Papias claimed that Mark had never heard Christ (Jmmanuel). Mark was an interpreter of Peter and he listened carefully

---

[161] Matt Slick, (2008 Document), When were the gospels written and by whom? Accessed 1/13/20. https://carm.org/when-were- gospels-written-and-whom.

of what Peter said when preaching. Mark's authorship is proposed as being between A.S. 55 to A.D. 70. [162]

**Luke** was not on scene to be an eyewitness to the events of Jesus (Jmmanuel's life). Luke was a companion of Paul who was not an eyewitness to the life of Christ (Jmmanuel).[163]

**Luke** existed as a single-book in 140CE when it was used by Marcion, and this early version was anonymous. There are some major edits in later versions, especially involving the insertion of the virgin-birth in Luke 2:33 and Luke 2:48. Later versions were "padded out" with extra inserted text, and had enough text added at the end that it had become known as the <u>Acts of the Apostles</u> and was included independently as the fifth book in the New Testament. [164]

**John** is a possible author of the so-called Gospel of John as well as the book of Revelation. Yet there is debate as to another possible individual known as "John the Elder." [165] Numerous scholars "consider it to be unlikely that John wrote anything, since he was known to be an unlettered man. Tradition further identifies John with the otherwise unnamed figure in the Gospel of John known as the beloved disciple. The fate of John is unknown. Some traditions state that he lived to an old age in Ephesus; others, that he was martyred early in life as had his brother." [166] John was the last to be written and there are some

---

[162] Ibid.

[163] Vexen Crabtree, (2015, Document), "Who Wrote the four Gospels of the New Testament? An Introduction to Matthew, Mark, Luke and John," accessed 1/13/20, http://www.humanreligions.info/gospels.html.

[164] Wikipedia (2016) s.v. "When were the New Testament authors born?" https://en.wikipedia.org.wiki.Gospel.

[165] Readers Digest, (1994, 233), *Who's Who in the Bible,* United States of America.

[166] Vexen Crabtree, (2015, Document), "Who Wrote the four Gospels of the New Testament? An Introduction to Matthew, Mark, Luke and John," accessed 1/13/20, http://www.humanreligions.info/gospels.html.

complications about it that give grave doubt about its authenticity such as the fact that the latest fragment of the gospel from 125 CE shows Jesus (Jmmanuel) speaking in a completely different language, sentence structure, and style compared to the other gospels. Not only that, but it contradicts the other gospels on almost every point of history. [167]

The reliability of having an author as a side-by-side companion from day to day to record events is unlikely. Consider the following on "Who Wrote the Four Gospels

of the New Testament, "An Introduction to Matthew, Mark, Luke, and John." [168]

1. In the early centuries of Christianity, there were over 200 Christian gospels in circulation.
2. It was decided by the early Church that there should be just four Gospels to correspond to the four winds, four points on the compass, and four corners of the temple.
3. Numerous stories in the Gospels are copied from Greek god-man legends.
4. All though the Gospels are named after a supposed author, they are all originally anonymous.
5. None of the Gospels contain a first-person account.
6. Justin Martyr in his writings approximately 150-60 CE quotes verses from the Gospels but never indicates what Gospels they came from. They were collectively thought of as ' 'Memories of the Apostles.'
7. Mark was written between 60 and 80 CE. When writings were compared, Matthew copied 92% of Mark; Luke, written after

---

[167] Ibid.

[168] Billy Meier, "Contact 003, lines 39-42" *They Fly*, February 8, 1975. http://www.theyfly.com/.

93 CE shows that 54% of it was copied. This shows that they both used the same text.

8. The Gospels went through times of alteration, editing and manipulation. The truth is that of the thousands of fragments of the Gospels, no two copies of the same text are actually exactly the same. It is claimed that entire chapters were added by later editors.

9. Because of difficulty in trying to work out 'what had happened,' it is obvious that by 120 CE there is no consistent record of Jesus' (Jmmanuel's) life.

The point of confronting the invalid authenticity of the Gospels is to demonstrate the confusion in the authorships of the various Gospels, to bring out the fact that there were manuscripts that were false, incomplete, changed or deleted without dates or other pertinent information to substantiate their completeness or authenticity.

However, the Talmud of Jmmanuel is solid in identifying the author, Judas Ischkerioth, his reliability as being a side- by-side personage, and his writing in the Old Aramaic language.

It is known that the Judeo/Christian Scripture is in a cobbled up state with a huge amount of ancient extraterrestrial interaction that is missing from history and in particular Biblical history, the erroneous lineage of Jmmanuel, inaccurate dating of the books, unknown or presumed authors of them, the lack of or non-existent oversight by a deity in the compilation of what was "authorized" Scripture and what was not and the so-called miracles that are explained through the natural application of science.

## The Crucifixion

The Crucifixion is the capstone of the Christian faith, but it truly does not end there. The Christian Faith, the Jewish Faith, and others that have identified themselves with what has become known as the

"God-believers" has been cobbled up in lies, cover-ups and omissions in the true account that extends far beyond the streets of Jerusalem and the Hills of Galilee.

Because of the doctrinal background on the matters of sin, atonement, forgiveness and eternal life, the TRUE STORY OF THE CRUCIFIXION will be hard to comprehend to those that have been raised in a conservative belief atmosphere. But, if you keep an open mind to the fact that there is verifiable truth to the account of Jmmanuel (aka Jesus) having survived the crucifixion, marrying, having children, and then traveling on to India, you will gain an immense insight into the lies that have been told about the crucifixion in the four gospels.

The Christian Bible tells us that Jmmanuel did not survive the crucifixion and was laid in a tomb for three days, after which it was declared that he rose, witnessed by brethren and subsequently was taken up into heaven.

First, we need to understand that Jmmanuel (aka Jesus) was not nailed to a cross as is commonly claimed by Christianity and others. The high spirit level known as Arahat Athersata, has stated that Jmmanuel was nailed to a "Y" type of wood configuration. There are many views on this matter as to whether it was a vertical pole, the typical cross that is vertical with a cross-beam, a "T" configuration or a "Y" formation. The authority in the matter should be the statement by the Arahat Athersata spirit level of the crucifixion on a "Y" formation of wood. The reason why this source of information is preferred is because of the human spirits at that level have "reached a certain spiritual and consciousness-related state of relative perfection and a correspondingly high and sound way of living." [169] This corresponds to a spirit level that is superior in the knowledge of happenings as well wisdom that cannot be fathomed in human comprehension.

---

[169] Billy Meier, (2016, 494-504), *Talmud of Jmmanuel*, Landesgruppe, Canada.

Continuing on with the crucifixion account, the Talmud of Jmmanuel continues with the record that after Jmmanuel cried out during a clap of thunder his head fell forward as he slipped into a state of "apparent death" which made those standing by think that he was truly dead. Joseph of Arimathea was granted Jmmanuel's body which he then placed in a tomb that was his own. The account in the Talmud of Jmmanuel tells us that there was a secret entrance in the back of the tomb cave that was unknown to the soldiers that had stood guard. The Talmud of Jmmanuel tells of how some of Jmmanuel's friends from India, who were staying in Jerusalem, had nursed Jmmanuel back to health through herbs, salves, and juices for three days and three nights. On the third day, Jmmanuel was of full strength and able to leave the cave through the secret back entrance with his friends. [170]

Jmmanuel spoke to his disciples one last time on the shore of the Sea of Galilee and told them to go to a hill in Galilee where He had spoken before. He spoke of going to India to give the old 'teaching of the prophets,' Creation, refraining from proselytizing, the lack of knowledge and wisdom in human beings, how to have victory in one's life, discernment over good and evil, conforming one's life to the Laws and Recommendations and living within one's own spirit (consciousness). He also spoke of seeking and finding the truth, gaining a higher spiritual level, and the definition of pure love. His final words were prophetic as he spoke of a new prophet appearing in "two times a thousand years" and teaching others to be new proclaimers. [171]

The really unique part of this true story is not Jmmanuel leaving Earth by being caught up into the clouds as the Bible would have mankind believe, but the descending of a Plejaren beamship that Jmmanuel went into and then ascended back into the sky. [172]

---

[170] Billy Meier, (2016, 505-512), *Talmud of Jmmanuel*, Landesgruppe, Canada.

[171] Billy Meier, (2016, 514), *Talmud of Jmmanuel*, Landesgruppe, Canada.

[172] Billy Meier, (2016, 514-560), *Talmud of Jmmanuel*, Landesgruppe, Canada.

Dr. Ron Pleune

A short time later a Plejaren beamship delivered Jmmanuel in the nearby land of Syria, where he took up residence in Damascus, Syria, for two years. During this time period, Jmmanuel spoke to Thomas and Judas Ischkerioth. Jmmanuel also met Saulus but did not identify himself to Saulus. Jmmanuel remained in Damascus for thirty days and then traveled on to India with his mother, his brother Thomas and Judas Ischkerioth. Jmmanuel taught about Creation and the Spirit within the human body which are governed by the "laws of the spirit of the Creation." <u>Jmmanuel continued with the</u> explaining of the "period of slumber of Creation," the concept of "oneness" and the fact that there is no such validity in the teaching of a so-called "trinity" as taught in Christianity. After Jmmanuel spoke to a group of individuals from a society called the 'Association of the Essenes' he traveled east with a caravan and taught about Creation, the home of the Spirit in the human being, as well as the deepening of knowledge regarding love, the truth, discernment (logic), freedom, peace, wisdom, and harmony. [173]

According to the Epilogue and Explanation, Jmmanuel's trip to India took several years. In the 'outermost spurs of the western Himalayas' his mother became sick and died when Jmmanuel was approximately 38 years old. After his mother's death, he continued to what is known today as Kashmir, India, where he continued to teach. At the age of 45, he married, had several children, and settled in Srinagar in Kashmir, India. At age 111, he passed away and was buried there. Judas Ischkerioth passed away at age 90 and was buried near Srinagar. Jmmanuel's oldest son, Joseph, continued writing about his father, left India, and returned to Jerusalem after a three-year journey where he started a family who also had descendants. He eventually passed away in Jerusalem after hiding the Scroll (later becoming the Talmud of Jmmanuel) in a tomb, as was discovered in 1963 by Billy Meier and Isa Rashid. [174]

---

[173] Billy Meier, (2016, 562-564), *Talmud of Jmmanuel*, Landesgruppe, Canada.

[174] Billy Meier, (2002, Document), *Questions to Billy Meier- Answered*, http://www25.brinkster.com/chancede/Answers.html.

Not only does the Talmud of Jmmanuel testify of Jmmanuel's life after being staked and surviving the ordeal, but other sources do also, as listed here.

Compiler's Note: This section is included in support of the FIGU publication 'The Talmud of Jmmanuel', a key aspect of the Billy Meier case. Regarding Jmmanuel's death in Srinagar, Kashmir, India at the age of 115 in 111 A.D., see the following German-language Contact Report excerpt: http://www.figu.org/de/figu/bulletin/45/leserfragen.htm.

Christ in Kashmir
Aziz Kashmiri
1973/1983/1984/1988/1994/1998 Roshni Publications, 160 pages + 6 pages appendices
http://www.tombofjesus.Com/BookStore.htm#CIK

The Christ of India
Swami Nirmalananda Giri
2006 (?) Atma Jyoti Ashram [Borrego Springs, California, USA], 48 pages
http://www.atmajyoti.org/pdfs/christ of india.pdf http://www.atmajyoti.org/spirwrit-the christ of india.asp

http://www.thaiexotictreasures.com/christ of india essene christianity.html

Countdown To Sabbath: Did Jesus Die On The Cross? Chandrani Samuel
1998 Cosmo Publications, 233 pages, ISBN 8170208513

Deliverance from the Cross Muhammad Zafarullah Khan 1978

Did Jesus Die? [BBC4-TV program May 1, 2006; produced in 2003]
http://forum.sharevirus.com/viewtopic.php?t=21807
[excerpt with Urdu subtitles, titled "Did Jesus Die On The Cross?"]
http://www.thelastoutpost.com/site/1389/default.aspx

Dr. Ron Pleune

The Fifth Gospel
Fida Hassnain and Dahan Levi
1988 Rima Publishing House, 320 pages

From Kashmir To Palestine
Paramesa Choudhury
1996 P. Choudhury (New Delhi), ISBN 8190012754, 370 pages

Himalaya: A Monograph
Nicholas Roerich, Francis R. Grant, Mary Siegrist,
George Grebenstchikoff and Ivan Narodny
1926 Brentano's, 210 pages

In Search Of Jesus, Last Starchild of the Old Silk Road: a journey into understanding historical religious conflicts
Suzanna Olsson
2004 AuthorHouse, ISBN 1418479861, 205 pages
http://www.jesus-kashmir-tomb.com/

In The World's Attic: Jesus In Leh (Kashmir)
Henrietta Sands Merrick
1931 G.P. Putnam's Sons, 259 pages

Jesus Among the Lost Sheep
Aziz A. Chaudhary
1992 Islam International Publication, 141 pages, ISBN 1853724963

Jesus and Moses Are Buried in India, Birthplace of Abraham and the Hebrews!
Gene D. Matlock
1991 Geo-Mind Publications, ISBN 0962773905
19?? iUniverse Inc., ISBN 0595127711
2000, Author's Choice Press, ISBN 0595127711

Jesus Died in Kashmir: Jesus, Moses and the Ten Lost Tribes of Israel

Andreas Faber Kaiser
1977 Gordon& Cremonesi, 184 pages, ISBN 0860330419

Jesus in Heaven on Earth: Journey of Jesus to Kashmir, His Preaching to the Lost Tribes of Israel, and Death and Burial in Srinagar
Khwaja Nazir Ahmad
1952/1956/1972/1988/1998 Woking Muslim Mission& Literary Trust, 471 pages, ISBN 0913321605
1999 Ahamadiyya Anjuman Ishaat Islam Lahore, ISBN 0913321605
http://aaiil.org/text/books/others/khwajanazirahmad/jesusin heavenonearth/jesusmheavenonearth.shtml#txt

Jesus In India
K.R.K. Sarma

Jesus In India: being an account of Jesus' escape from death on the cross and of his journey to India
Hazrat Mirza Ghulam Ahmad
1978 The London Mosque
1989 Islam International Publications Ltd., ISBN 1853721964

1944/1991 Nazarat Nashr-o-Ishaat 103 pages http://www.geocities.com/Athens/Delphi/1340/jesus in in dia.htm

http://www.alislam.org/books/jesus-in-india/

Jesus In India: Jesus' Deliverance from the Cross& Journey to India
2003 Nazarat Nashro Ishaat, 160 pages

Jesus In India: A Reexamination Of Jesus' Asian Traditions In The Light Of Evidence Supporting Reincarnation

James Deardorff
2002 International Scholars Publications, 315 pages, ISBN 1883255368

2002 Rowman& Littlefield, 315 pages, ISBN 1883255368

Jesus in India: A Review of the World Literature (18991999)
Dr. Tahir Ijaz and Qamar Ijaz Ph.D.
http://www.tombofjesus.com/BookReviews.htm
http://www.alislam.org/sunrise/sunrise2003-4.pdf

Jesus In Kashmir
Dr. Robert "Bob" Holt
http://j esusinkashmir.com/
http://www.healthark.com/imedia/indexa.htm

Jesus In Kashmir
http://www.goacom.com/overseas-digest/Religion/jesus- in-kashmir.htm

Jesus in the Valley of Kashmir
Abdul Mannan Khalifa

Jesus, Last King of Kashmir: Life After the Crucifixion Suzanne Olsson
2006 BookSurge Publishing, 316 pages, ISBN

1419611755

Jesus Lived in India: His unknown life before& after the Crucifixion
Holger Kersten
1994 Harper-Collins UK, 264 pages, ISBN 1852305509

http://www.siliconindia.com/books/newbooks/booksdetails.asp?bid=560
Synopsis by Dr Ramesh Manocha& Anna Potts
http://www.sol.com.au/kor/7 01.htm
http://www.spinninglobe.net/jesusinindia.htm

Jesus Messiah, Isha Masih, Issa Mashiha, Hazrat Issa, Yuzu Asaph, Yesu, Esus, Jesus Christ http://www.algonet.se/~hermesat/issa.htm

Jesus of India
Maurice Entwistle
"Jesus Of The East" by Simon Price, Fortean Times#183 (May 2004):

http://www.forteantimes.com/articles/183_jesuseast1.shtml

http://www.forteantimes.com/articles/183_jesuseast2.shtml

http://www.forteantimes.com/articles/183_jesuseast3.shtml

http://www.forteantimes.com/articles/183_jesuseast4.shtml

http://www.forteantimes.com/articles/183_jesuseast5.shtml

Jesus' Tomb in India: The Debate on His Death and Resurrection
Paul C. Pappas

1991 Jain Publishing Co., 200 pages, ISBN 0895819465

King Of Travelers: Jesus' Lost Years In India
Edward T. Martin
1999 The Twiggs Company, 245 pages, ISBN 0967240832;
Also published as an eBook CD-ROM in
2004: http://www.theyfly.com/products/products.htm

The Life of Saint Issa: Best of the Sons of Men
Nicolas Notovitch (translator)
http://reluctant-messenger.com/issa.htm

Rauzabal and other Mysteries of Kashmir
Mohammad Yasin
1972 Kesar Publishers

Saving the Savior: Did Christ Survive the Crucifixion?

Dr. Ron Pleune

Abubakr Ben Ishmael Salahuddin
2001 Jammu Press, 408 pages, ISBN 0970828012

A Search For The Historical Jesus: From Apocryphal, Buddhist, Islamic& Sanskrit Sources
Professor Fida Hassnain
1994 Gateway Books, 244 pages, ISBN 0946551995
2003 Access Publishers Network, ISBN 0946551995

Survival of the Crucifixion: Traditions of Jesus within Islam, Buddhism, Hinduism and Paganism
James Deardorff
http://www.tjresearch.info/legends.htm

The Talmud Of Jmmanuel: "Did Christ Survive the Cross?"
2001 International UFO Congress; 4th International UFO

Congress Summer
Seminar, 9/17/01 Laughlin NV; lectures/presentations by Wendelle Stevens, Edward T. Martin, Prof. James Deardorff, and Dr. Dietmar Rothe; 4.5 hour 2-tape set [tape numbers 362-A, 362-B]; UFO Collector Series Volume 362; "Need To Know" imprint/series; e-mail: ufocongress@msn.com
Dietmar Ro Compiler's Note: This section is included in support of the FIGU publication 'The Talmud of Jmmanuel', a key aspect of the Billy Meier case. Regarding Jmmanuel's death in Srinagar, Kashmir, India at the age of 115 in 111 A.D., see the following German-language Contact Report excerpt: http://www.figu.org/de/figu/bulletin/45/leserfragen.htm

The Zoh Show- Jesus' Lost Years in India- Edward T Martin (6-23-00)
http://www.yousendit.com/transfer.php?action=download&ufid=D18B86DD1829A931the presentation/lecture:
http://www.avilabooks.com/Jmmanuel.htm

http://www.avilabooks.com/Jmmanuel1.htm
http://www.avilabooks.com/Jmmanuel2.htm
http://www.avilabooks.com/Jmmanuel3.htm
http://www.avilabooks.com/Jmmanuel4.htm

The Tomb of Jesus
Sufi Mutiur Rahman Bengalee [various name spellings: Matiur, Rehman]
1946 The Moslem Sunrise Press

The Tomb of Jesus Christ
http://www.tombofjesus.com/
The Unknown Life of Jesus Christ
Nicolas Notovitch
1894 Indo-American Book Company, 191 pages
1907 Progressive Thinker Publishing House, xxxii + 156 pages
1974 Gordon Press, 288 pages, ISBN 0879680733
1990/1996 Tree Of Life Publications, 62 pages, ISBN 0960285016
http://www.sacred-texts.com/chr/ulj c/index.htm
http://www.atmajyoti.org/sw unknown life.asp

Where did Jesus Die?
Maulana J.D. Shams
1988 Nazir Dawat-o-Tabligh, 199 pages, ISBN 1853721905
2002 Nazir Dawat-o-Tabligh, 136 pages, ISBN 1853721905

The Zoh Show- Jesus' Lost Years in India- Edward T Martin (6-23-00)

http://www.yousendit.com/transfer.php?action=download&ufid=D18B86DD1829A931

# Chapter 5

# Victorious Living without God

### Moving Ahead in Truth

The topics that have been covered so far may seem unbelievable, hard to comprehend, and even going against what the reader has been taught or influenced by. Keeping an open mind to the revelations of the Truth brought most recently by the onset of more exposure to ufology is the key to understanding the truths herein. There is a massive amount of information that has not been presented so far that can be obtained from the website *Theyfly.com*. I have only touched upon a few topics that strike home in the Christian belief that should whet your appetite for more information about ufology, the history of mankind and our universe.

For some readers, the here and now is important...that is to say just living from day to day, which is known as just surviving the daily humdrum of human existence.

However, if you search the website of Billy Meier and see the immense information on Earth's history and other planets as well as predictions and prophecies that have been announced by Billy Meier that have been fulfilled it will most assuredly amaze you. It is fascinating to learn about the scientific approach to space travel, the creation and evolution of planets, comets and the struggles of humans on other planets with genetic manipulation and social issues which in some cases resulted in war and the movement of mass populations to other planets such as Mars and Earth.

Well, they had their challenges in life and are no different in that respect than we have here on Earth. As pointed out earlier in this writing, the Plejaren are 3,500 years ahead of us in technology, yet they have guidelines in their society that guide them in harmonious ways for the most part as described below,[175] and. [176]

Family

- There are some Plejaren males who are not married, others to just one woman.
- Each family (of a maximum of 5 persons: husband, wife, three children)
- Each wife has her own house and parcel of land (about 100 x 100 m).
- In the case of where women and children live together, each wife/family still has her own residence where she can go to if she wishes.
- The man is visiting his several families (if there are several) on a regular basis. But, of course, he is always willing and ready to visit all his families anytime if there is a problem, and the wives are there for him too if he has a problem, etc.
- The man can marry up to four women Economy
- Non-monetary
- Robot-assisted manufacturing
- Poverty eradicated
- Food, energy and housing are free

---

[175] Billy Meier, (2013 Document), *Planet Erra,* http://www.meiersaken.info/Planet_Erra.html.

[176] Billy Meier, *Goblet of the Truth.* (Canada: FIGU-Landsgruppe Canada, 2015, IX).

- One single government exists
- Use no land vehicles at all
- Each dwelling has its own water and power supply
- Animals never belong in residential living spaces, where humans live
- Daily nutrition of the population is fruits as well as types of grains, potatoes, berries and all sorts of vegetables grown
- Plejarens live on mineral and vegetable, as well as animal products
- Each family, or other housing units on these plots of land, establishes their own fruit-, vegetable-, herb and flower garden

Relationships- Personal and Social

- Monogamy and polygamy exist- one man to many women but not the other way around
- No homosexual or bisexual exists because this genetic disorder has been eradicated through genetic manipulation
- Virtually no incompatible couples
- Divorce is not allowed
- No religion

Life on Erra appears to be pretty organized and running smoothly **without God**. The Plejaren and the Universe of extraterrestrials recognizes that there is no God as shown earlier in this work. However, peace did not happen overnight as was noted previously with the Plejaren (previously noted as Lyrans from the Galaxy of Lyra). There were wars that ensued as noted in Contact Report 251 and 70 as well as mischief with Gene Manipulation and dominance by Over-Lords. God did not have a part in the extraterrestrial lives; it was purely their human nature just as it is in the humans here on Earth with selfishness, greed and lust for power, hidden agendas, dominance and to put mankind under servitude and slavery both physically and mentally.

The question then is "what changed them to living in a positive way?" The answer is found in the Introduction of the Goblet of the Truth that embodies the teachings of the seven prophets which in particular is the Teaching of the Truth, Teaching of the Spirit and Teaching of the Life. These teachings were passed down through oral communication but were never written down in a one volume composite down through the millennia until the last of the seven prophets, namely Eduard Albert Meier, who was also nicknamed "Billy, as well as "BEAM," which stands for Billy Eduard Albert Meier. Embodied within the Teaching of the Truth, Teaching of the Spirit and Teaching of the Life is what is called the Laws and Recommendations. The Laws are the scientific laws that govern the tangible (that which can be seen and grasped) and intangible (such as gravity, radiation, etc.) that were created by the Spirit-Energy of Creation and are unchangeable. The Recommendations are the teachings of the Life which gives guidance to all human life for private and public living. [177]

The credibility of the history of the cosmos is found in the revelations made by humans from the Pleiades which are some 80 light years beyond the Pleiades star formation. This was revealed by extraterrestrial humans that began explaining to Billy (Eduard) Albert Meier facets about the universe and all that is in it. This information is true and reliable based on their actual human existence and appearance in living tangible form to Billy Meier and whose ships have been witnessed by hundreds of people since 1942. Their existence is also verified by the information the Plejaren have given to Billy that are scientific and have been verified since 1942. Mr. Meier has his contacts with the Plejaren cataloged on the website theyfly.com. Some are listed but not disclosed due to the sensitive nature of the topic involving person (s) and information.

The Recommendations are exactly as it is stated "Recommendations" that one may choose to obey or not. No penalty is involved such as the Christian religion teaches that one can lose the blessings of God or

---

[177] Billy Meier, *Goblet of the Truth*. (Canada: FIGU-Landsgruppe Canada, 2015, XI).

*Dr. Ron Pleune*

not be guaranteed eternal life. The "Recommendations" state various warnings and blessings for following them which will result in the disappointment, discouragement and sorrow that come in daily living to ones-self and even the relationship (s) one may have with another.

The groundwork for the Laws and Recommendations is found in the seven pillars of wisdom which are love, truth, fairness, knowledge, logic, respect, and honor. These in turn feed the seven basic powers of humans; strength, rationality, intellect, self-discipline, self-control, selfachievement and fearlessness. [178]

As said previously, the Laws and Recommendations are embodied in the Goblet of the Truth and cover all situations that people have. Here is a sampling of them as found online for the Index to the Goblet of the Truth. [179]

Abuse, Accountability, Achievement, Adoption, Adultery, Alcohol, Animals, Argument, Behavior, Benevolence, Business, Cause and Effect, Change, Children, Choice, Conduct, Consciousness, Death, Deception, Delusion and many more…in fact as of the writing of this book there are 3,3800 entries!

The topics are arranged alphabetically which allows a person to quickly scroll down to the topic of their interest and then note the page number, chapter and verse for follow-up of it in the Goblet of the Truth.

All this is fine, but what about having a victorious life without God… or for that matter referring to a Bible?

Let's go through an example of how this is done by keeping the process simple.

---

[178] Pleune D.R.E, Ronald, (2016 Document), "Index for the Goblet of the Truth," *They Fly*

[179] Billy Meier, *Goblet of the Truth*. (Canada: FIGU-Landsgruppe Canada, 2015, 515).

1. Pick a topic
2. Read it through several times so that you understand its meaning.
3. Follow the guideline of Education, Rationality and Logic. [180]

    A. **Educate** yourself regarding the subject that you are confronted with.

    B. **Rationality-** list what options are available.
    Ask key questions below.

    Do they interact?

    Is there a cost to them materialistically, psychologically, socially, monetarily or positional?

    Are there corrective measures and what do they entail?

    Are there other verses in the Goblet of the Truth that go deeper to help me?

    Will I need the help of others to conquer what I am facing?

    C. **Logic-** use it to choose from the options you've looked at to give yourself the greatest advantage toward self-discipline and effective compliance day to day.

4. Pray to your spirit, which is within your mind, and ask for help (see section on the Spirit) in the performance of a positive action or in the case of a warning or guide to stop doing something ask for a way to block an unwanted action or thought.

Your Spirit will also help you through the means of "self-talk" toward the goal of positive action to accomplish something or to stop a destructive nature by promoting selfawareness toward a positive action.

---

[180] Billy Meier, *Goblet of the Truth*. (Canada: FIGU-Landsgruppe Canada, 2015, 509, 104).

Dr. Ron Pleune

At the heart of this is the fact that you are the one to determine what course of action you take, if any. You become your own guide and self-counselor because you will have taken the time out to work-out a matter. You see, this is your life, not your parents or siblings. If you are married, it will be a joint outcome because the same process is used whether you are single or not. The Goblet of the Truth is explicit on this matter as the Index to the topics of Responsibility and Accountability are spelled out for you in the "**short sampling**" shown below. For a more comprehensive list go to *theyfly.com* website, on the left side of the site a short distance down the page "click" on the sentence *Topic Index for the Goblet of the Truth*, wait for it to download on your screen and then choose the topic of your choice. Once you have picked your topic of interest, click on the "*Goblet of the Truth*" on the *theyfly.com* website to examine the verse (s) that you chose.

Page Ch. Verse

| | | | |
|---|---|---|---|
| Responsible fullness- living in accordance with Creational Laws& Recommendations to a fresh, joyful& pure activity | 567 | 28 | 455-456 |
| **Responsibility- each shall take responsibility for themselves, not onto others nor gods or tin gods** | 73 | 2 | 401 |
| Responsibility- be responsible at all times so that you take the way of the Truth | 209 | 6 | 76 |

| | | | |
|---|---|---|---|
| Responsibility- your personal decision on how to think and act | 173 | 5 | 34 |
| **Responsibility- you alone have the power to do good and better things for yourself** | 327 | 11 | 59 |

| | | | |
|---|---|---|---|
| Responsibility- creational energy& power is given to all& used by your own will | 501 | 28 | 65-66 |
| **Responsibility- each person has for their existence, deeds and efforts** | 113 | 3 | 236 |

| | | | |
|---|---|---|---|
| Accountability- comes to you sooner or later in one way or another | 345 | 15 | 20 |
| Accountability- personal | 273 | 8 | 35-36 |
| Accountability- personal for your thoughts and values | 465 | 25 | 260-265 |
| Accountability- for unlawful actions | 231 | 7 | 4-8 |
| Accountability- in your conscience and through social jurisdiction | 205 | 6 | 54 |

| | | | |
|---|---|---|---|
| Free will- everyone decides to follow the Truth or not | 213 | 6 | 97 |
| Free will- changing the course of your thoughts and feelings according to your free choosing | 535 | 28 | 251-263 |
| Free will- choice based on insight (intellect) and true discernment (rationality) | 373 | 20 | 18 |
| Free will- connected with fine-fluidal of the nature of individuality, consciousness, selfdetermination. | 531 | 28 | 231-234 |
| Free will- deficiency of it | 529 | 28 | 221-223 |
| Free will- determines the process of selfdevelopment | 533 | 28 | 247-248 |

Dr. Ron Pleune

| Free will- search everything and decide the whole matter | 381 | 21 | 12-14 |
| --- | --- | --- | --- |
| Free will- to determine what is truth and what is untruth | 207 | 6 | 63-64 |
| Free will- guard it- or you could be led astray from the Truth | 219 | 6 | 123-125 |
| Free will- how to gain it | 529 | 28 | 224- 22 |
|  | Pg. | Ch. | Verse |
| Free will- includes your free decision- and determination-possibility | 529 | 28 | 216-217 |
| Free will- is not influenced by the stars, karma or guidance via powers of a god/idol/human being | 529 | 28 | 218 |
| Free will- its relationship to cause and effect | 531 | 28 | 241 |
| Free will- leads to success in following the Laws and Recommendations | 359 | 19 | 9 |

Responsibility and Accountability are driven by **Free Will**, a sampling of the topic of Free Will is listed below. You choose your schedule for the day, you choose what chores you wish to accomplish, you choose when to go to the store, you choose whom you will date and you choose all that happens during your day and how you interface with others... not God!!!!!!!

The Goblet of the Truth states that through your free will, you are the master of your own life as referenced below.

| Master- of your life through the real truth | 27 | 2 | 186 |
| --- | --- | --- | --- |
| Master- you are your own master | 313 | 10 | 50 |

| | | | |
|---|---|---|---|
| Master- you determine for yourselves benevolence or malevolence | 223 | 6 | 149 |

| | | | |
|---|---|---|---|
| Mastery of the life- through the understanding of the creational Laws& Recommendations | 383 | 22 | 14 |

## Your Own Decision

Ultimately the DECISION you make through your FREE WILL regarding your life personally and socially will determine your RESPONSIBILITY and ACCOUNTABILITY.

"Truly, you always have the free decision and the free determination at the beginning of each matter, as well as the free will to decide where to and in which direction you want to direct everything through your thoughts, feelings, actions and deeds and through your activity; but you do not think at all or only vaguely about this, which is why you cannot realize and understand the effects, i.e. the destiny out of the causes which you create yourselves; and out of your not-understanding regarding this you assume then that the destiny that strikes you is either earned or unearned and furthermore brought onto you through your fellow human beings some higher might because you refuse to understand that you yourselves are the former of your own destiny which you bring about yourselves and which has nothing to do with the destiny that acts from the outside and which is the result out of foreordinations over which you have no might." [181]

And if you look at the Creation-given energy and its power, then be conscious that it is only up to your thoughts and the there-out resulting feelings as well as up to your decision and will whether you want to bring forth good or evil through this immense and in itself neutral-positive- equalized energy

---

[181] Billy Meier, *Goblet of the Truth*. (Canada: FIGU-Landsgruppe Canada, 2015, 499, 55).

and power; truly, it is through your decision that the good or evil is given to you only, depending on what furthering or ruin-bringing thoughts and feelings you form in yourselves and bring into effect. [182]

"And yet the only things that help you to make the right decision and to succeed in choosing the right action are the cognition (rationality) and true discernment (intellect) when you connect yourselves with the truthly truth that proves its mightiness in all things and in all decisions; without use of the truth, cognition (rationality) and true discernment (intellect) are just as insignificant (useless) as smoke that dissipates in the air, because truly cognition (rationality) and true discernment (intellect) can only effectuate (create) things of reality if they determine the truth according to its rightness and use it according to the truth (in a right wise), whether by thoughts and feelings, speaking (words) or actions, page 353, chapter 17, verse 4." [183]

Now you can live VICTORIOUSLY WITHOUT GOD!!!

## Dealing with Rejection

Rejection is one of the toughest feelings that can be felt whether it's a job interview, friendship gone bad, marriage that bottomed out…or whatever makes you feel down and out because others have turned their backs against you. It's like the Civil War where it was brother against brother and the division that the Civil War brought is felt deeply in some parts of the southern United States even today.

Amongst the deeply religious groups or persons you may be on the receiving end of harsh words and negative treatment… especially from those that are Conservative or what is called Fundamentalist Christians,

---

[182] Billy Meier, *Goblet of the Truth*. (Canada: FIGU-Landsgruppe Canada, 2015, 353, v. 4).

[183] Billy Meier, *Goblet of the Truth*. (Canada: FIGU-Landsgruppe Canada, 2015, 61, v. 350).

there may be anger and even the cutting off of their association with you because they will think that they are "in the right." They are fundamentally insensitive even though the Christian Scripture instructs the Christian in word and deed to conduct themselves with integrity toward those that have an opposing view (s). One of the worst actions that a Christian can and has done (which I have witnessed) is the cutting off of family association. The Christian holds in their heart hurt and a "get you back" feeling that turns into outward action by <u>not letting</u> friends and relatives that have a nonChristian conviction communicate or visit with them.

This truly is a travesty against mankind because children hear their parent's harsh remarks and see how they act with cruelty towards others. As children grow up, they carry the negativity of their parents into other social arenas, and then they wonder why they can't get along with those of color, other beliefs, political differences and social preferences. The cancer of wrongful attitude had been planted... and has now been spread like seed in a fertile field.

What you need to consider and keep in mind is that they only know what they have been taught which is usually in their childhood years, and through the religious training of their denomination which may also be from a teacher who is bent on prejudice, prejudice, prejudice. I have invited many people to go out late at night and perform "signaling" with my spotlight and when I tell them it is for contacting extraterrestrial humans the air turns ice cold many times. The question we need to ask here is "how should those that hold to the Truth of the Laws and Recommendations respond so that we can remain friends with them… the best that we can. The key to the answer is the following.

**Relax-** In any type of approach whether one on one, a small group or even a large audience a person may feel uptight and nervous. This is a time when you need to focus on every word, how you come across with your approach and even how you present yourself in body language. The Goblet of the Truth is so practical and exciting that a person can easily get exuberant when talking to someone about the Billy Meier Story and that's when it's time to take a deep breath of air and organize your thoughts so that you don't run ahead of what you are trying to get across to the other person. Taking a moment to settle down is also important because you may encounter a push-back from people. Sometimes they will object to just about everything that comes out of your mouth.

When you feel anxiety, free yourself from it through the contemplation of good and free thoughts and feelings. [184]

**Refrain** from arguing- Plan your revelation of the Truth carefully. Don't try to memorize everything...I guarantee you will forget most of it due to your heightened expectations. A good verbal approach is to ask questions and allow the other person to come back with their questions. Arguing gets you nowhere. As you speak to more and more people you will feel more at ease which will allow your words to come out in a non-confrontational manner. Bring along some literature from the website *theyfly.com* and let the proof within it be the convincing agent.

Anger rises when you cause people to be in rage toward you, it affects your thoughts, feelings and psyche toward sorrow. [185]

**Respond** in kindness/understanding- Sometimes when we want to get our point across so quickly and boldly that we actually end up running over our opponent. Be positive and happy so that the other person (s) will see your enthusiasm and joy, especially when it comes to explaining the Laws and Recommendations. Inform them that there are many UFO groups in the world that look to the skies but that they become stagnant due to not learning about themselves and mankind in day to day living.

---

[184] Billy Meier, *Goblet of the Truth*. (Canada: FIGU-Landsgruppe Canada, 2015, 107, v. 206).

[185] Billy Meier, *Goblet of the Truth*. (Canada: FIGU-Landsgruppe Canada, 2015, 259, v. 163-164).

*God, The Grandest Illusion*

Be sensitive regarding your behavior- do not be outrageous (presumptuous) in your words when speaking to fellow human beings. [186]

**Re-think** your approach- It may be time to back off and try another day. Remember, you don't have to win them over this very moment. They are not going to hell if they don't respond in a positive manner. Most of the time, after I speak with them, I try and set a day that they can go out with me to do signaling for UFO and I am able to weave the Billy Meier Story in with UFO that fly over us. Using that approach I convince my guest (s) that the Plejaren are real and friendly. If nothing comes about with this meeting, don't lose heart, there will be a next time or another opportunity to go over the Billy Meier notes.

It is not effective in forcing it upon the unknowing ones nor attack their thoughts and feelings. [187]

You know that what you have learned from the Goblet of the Truth is rich in guidance as well as relying on selfprayer for your Spirit to help you in being truthful and upright in your life, but rejection seems to cut across life's strings and make you feel as though your pet rock is even against you.

Rejection through various forms of persecution will come from those that are unwilling to acknowledge the real Truth of the Laws and Recommendations. The Goblet of the Truth states the following.

"And those who are without equitableness (unfair ones/irresponsible ones/inequitable ones) and the believers, as well as the priests of gods and tin gods, will not cease earlier their evil deeds of **fighting** against those who are knowing of the truth, **insulting** them, **slandering** them or **slaying** them or having them killed (murdered) in dastardly fashion; **and they will not**

---

[186] Billy Meier, *Goblet of the Truth*. (Canada: FIGU-Landsgruppe Canada, 2015, 31, v. 213).

[187] Billy Meier, *Goblet of the Truth*. (Canada: FIGU-Landsgruppe Canada, 2015, 59, v. 336).

**take an early repose** until they have made the ones who have knowledge of the truth defect to their belief and to their god or tin gods, even if they were able to do so, because it is not possible to get those who are knowing of the truth away from their true knowledge about the truth." [188]

Notice that those that disagree with the Laws and Recommendations will use verbal abuse and even physical action against those that accept and practice the Truth. The question that comes to mind is "who are the ones that are referred to in the previous sentence as being "those?" We once again find the answer in the Goblet of the Truth as follows.

"And for almost four thousand years, in which your great religions, sects, ideologies and philosophies and your catastrophic forms of politics have arisen, the basis of your Ausartungen (German meaning for a very bad get-out of the control of the good human nature) of all kinds and the turning away from the real truth of all truth and hence from the Creation Universal Consciousness and its laws and recommendations has become increasingly dreadful." [189]

We move on to the next question. "What is needed to accept the Truth and to live by it?" There is no God that will speak to you (as in the term inspiration), there is no savior by which you must receive a salvation of any kind through a prayer or religious rites of passage, a so-called obedience statement or a fulfillment of certain duties and/or practices. As the verse below states you cannot come to the knowledge of the Truth until you place yourself as Judge over yourself so that you examine everything that is unrightful within yourself and are firmly convinced in your connection and identity with the Truth, that is to say the Laws and Recommendations of Creation.

---

[188] Billy Meier, *Goblet of the Truth*. (Canada: FIGU-Landsgruppe Canada, 2015, 559, v. 400).

[189] Billy Meier, *Goblet of the Truth*. (Canada: FIGU-Landsgruppe Canada, 2015, 133, v. 92).

*God, The Grandest Illusion*

"Those amongst you, however, who are believers in gods and tin gods because you lend your ear to the priests of gods and priests of tin gods and other servants of gods and servants of tin gods, you cannot become ones who have knowledge of the truth until you place yourselves as judges over your own selves and above everything that is contentious in you so that you may turn to the truthteaching of the prophets and no longer have any doubts in yourselves about your decision to connect yourselves to the truth and to join this acquiescence (Forbearance)." [190]

The next question is "how do I continue day to day in the Truth?" There are certain things that must be learned that require repetition just as a sport of any type requires. This involves daily or periodical research and the application of basics that evolve into deeper understanding. The Goblet of the Truth puts it this way; "And the most important permanent activity that you shall work on is the building of the truth in yourselves, by gathering truthly knowledge and true wisdom, by means of which you create true love and freedom in yourselves and outside yourselves, as well as peace and consonance (harmony)." [191]

The final step is for you to follow the Truth. No one else can take your place or "pinch hit" for you. The responsibility is all yours, the accountability to put it into practice is all yours, yet there are other documents and "helps" that will give you a deeper understanding such as the Contact Reports, explanations from FIGU, writings of Billy Meier found on the *theyfly.com* website and the Talmud of Jmmanuel. There is also help through communicating with one of the 49 core group members as I do from time to time.

"However, exercise patience and learn so that you experience the truth and are able to decide between it and your belief (assumptions), because

---

[190] Billy Meier, *Goblet of the Truth*. (Canada: FIGU-Landsgruppe Canada, 2015, 339, v. 14).

[191] Billy Meier, *Goblet of the Truth*. (Canada: FIGU-Landsgruppe Canada, 2015, 247, v88b).

you alone are the true determiners over whether you want to open your ears to the truth or to the untruth." [192]

Once you have decided to claim and follow the Laws and Recommendations of the Truth, you would logically ask "what will I gain from it?" An inner garden of Truth as is described below!

"See, the truth is always with you, but you have to make it <u>your own, because simply the</u> presence of the truth does not bring any benefit (success) unless you use it; therefore, be connected to the truth and heed it when you direct your prayer to your inner world (consciousness), when you distribute your alms and when you make a considerable commitment (effort/interest/attention) to learning about the teaching of the truth, the teaching of the spirit, the teaching of the life; and if you have committed misdeeds in the past, then you free yourselves of them if you are turned towards the truth and recognize the things in their reality, thus you can **create a garden of the truth in yourselves through which streams of cognition, love, peace, freedom and consonance (harmony) flow**; however, anyone amongst you who falls away from this way of the truth and returns to the path of the unknowledgeness that is strewn with thorns, that human being is truly straying from the straight-way." [193]

## Dealing with Growth

There is an unbelievable list of topics in the Goblet of the Truth that will give you guidance in your daily life; just a small sample of topics beginning with "A" are listed below.

---

[192] Billy Meier, *Goblet of the Truth*. (Canada: FIGU-Landsgruppe Canada, 2015, 169, v. 26).

[193] Billy Meier, *Goblet of the Truth*. (Canada: FIGU-Landsgruppe Canada, 2015, 181, v. 76).

| | | |
|---|---|---|
| Absolution | Abuse | Accountability |
| Accusations | Achievement | |
| Admonishment | Adoption | Adultery |
| Adversaries | Affliction | |
| Afraid | Aging | Agitation |
| Agreements | Alcohol | |
| Alms | Angels | Anger |
| Animals | Answer | |
| Antichrist | Anxiety | Apologies |
| Argue | Arrogance | |

"And truly, on your way of cognition and of unfolding (evolution), you are walking alone in yourselves because it is in yourselves that you have to do the work of learning, the work of investigation (research), recognition and unfolding (evolution); from outside of yourselves you only have sight and hearing, and taste and touch, as well as the words and the teaching of the true prophets from which you can take (accomplish) everything that you have to investigate (research) and to recognize (see) in yourselves so that you may become knowing (conscious) and wise and therefore righteous (conscientious) and fair (responsible) and fulfill the Laws and Recommendations of the primal wellspring of all modesty (Creation)." [194]

What this paragraph is saying is that as you learn, meaning "unfolding of knowledge aka (evolution), no one else can make the inner change for you… just you. This will take some work through getting into the Goblet of the Truth and recognize what has to be changed on the inside of you for your personal growth (evolution). Your hands, eyes, ears, legs etc. are external, it's what is in your mind that needs to be changed to some greater or lesser degree so that you are conscious of

---

[194] 196Dr. George King/Richard Lawrence, (2019 Document) "UFOs in the Bible and the Vedas," accessed January 25, 2020, https://www.aetherius.org/evidence/ufos-in-the-bible-and-the- vedas/.

how you develop your thoughts and respond toward creating love, peace, freedom and harmony inside of you and then responding in word and deed with those same abilities to those around you.

Christianity refers to a change in a person's life as being of the heart and mind, yet if it were seen in the proper perspective of Education, Rationality and Logic, there is no such thing as a "change of heart." A "change of heart" is actually the process of using Education, Rationality and Logic within a person's MIND because the heart has nothing to do with it, the heart is an organ that does not think or keep anything hidden or in the archives of your life. The heart simply pumps blood.

## Dealing with Reality- the UFO Connection

The question that begs asking now is why mankind of today doesn't understand that down through thousands and thousands of years that alien humans have had a direct impact on life here on earth? It is because we have been influenced in the past through the following.

1. Genetic manipulation in creating errors in our lives.
2. We have been under alien human domination by what Earth humans call "God."
3. We do not have the knowledge of struggles, wars, and influences of cosmic life.
4. Due to Religious influence, we refuse to acknowledge alien activity in Biblical texts.
5. We refuse to acknowledge or have an open mind to the history of the Earth, Mars, etc.
6. We refuse to accept the fact that the Goblet of the Truth has been from time immemorial and that the Truths in it were given in an oral fashion initially because of the lack of those that had writing skills to write it down, this led to the stealing

of the Truths of the Laws and Recommendations which were transferred to Judeo-Christian writings.

7. The lack of understanding and vocabulary in Judeo-Christian times of expressing the technology of ufology as in the following cases.

II Kings 2:11 (KJV regarding Elijah and the Chariot of Fire.

Ezekiel 1 (KJV) regarding the wheels (UFO) that came down to Earth.

Ezekiel 10:9-11 (KJV) regarding the appearance of the wheels (UFO) that came down to Earth.

Ezekiel 10:16 (KJV): regarding the (UFO) "wheels that went by them."

Matthew 2:9 (KJV): regarding "the star (UFO)…went before them"

John 18:36 (KJV): per Jmmanuel "My kingdom is not of this world:"

Acts 9:3 (KJV): "…and suddenly a light from heaven flashed around him."

Zechariah 5:1-2 (KJV): regarding a flying scroll… length… width.

Ezekiel 1:4-5 (KJV): regarding fire flashing."as it were gleaming metal."

Ezekiel 1:4-5 (KJV) regarding "four living creatures… likeness of a man."

Genesis 6:1 (KJV): regarding (alien forces) emissaries of God that took the liberty of mating with women.

Psalm 68:17 (KJV): regarding "The chariots of God are twenty thousand," as being UFO.

Revelation 1:1-20 (KJV): regarding the sending of an angel (emissary by way of a UFO) to John.

> Isaiah 13:5 (KJV): regarding "from the end of heaven" outer reaches of the universe" and "weapons of his indignation to destroy the whole land (weapons of mass destruction) as seen on the UFO.

There are many more verses that speak of cosmic entities and situations/conditions/descriptions that were hard for the people of those times to relate to because they did not have the expansive knowledge and terminology in a portable dictionary like what we have today.

There are records of UFO in ancient India, which by the way confirm UFO in Biblical times in the Old Testament and New Testament that Jmmanuel received transportation from as told in the Talmud of Jmmanuel.

In India, the word for UFO is noted as a "flying celestial vehicle," or in the Sanskrit word "vimana." Below are some texts from the Ramayana which typifies the description of a UFO. [195]

*When morning dawned, Rama, taking the vimana Puspaka had sent him by Vivpishand, stood ready to depart. Selfpropelled was that car. It was large and finely painted.*

*That aerial and excellent vimana, going everywhere at will, is ready for thee. That vimana, resembling a bright cloud in the sky, is in the city of Lanka.*

The following is from the Bhagavata Purana, Book 4 and Chapter 12.

*As soon as the symptoms of his liberation were manifest, he saw a very beautiful vimana coming down from the sky, as if the brilliant full moon were coming down, illuminating all the ten directions…*

---

[195] Cristian Violatti (2018 Document), "The Vedas," Accessed January 25, 2020, https://www.ancient.eu/The_Vedas/.

*While Dhruva Maharajah was passing through space, he gradually saw all the planets of the Solar System, and on the path, he saw all the demi-gods in their vimanas showering flowers upon him like rain...*

*Beyond that region, he achieved the transcendental situation of permanent life in the planet where Lord Vishnu lives.*

These quotes from India are of utmost importance since they are another testament to the reality of UFO!! The Vedas were written between 1500 and 1000 BCE in

Sanskrit writing. [196] Even an ancient Sanskrit from India tells of a UFO visit in 4,000 B.C. [197]

The question now is "what about the UFO seen today and how does it interface with our lives and the message for us today?"

The answer to that question is found in the "Talmud of Jmmanuel", Chapter 4, and Verses 50 through 52. Judas

Ischkerioth writes that once Jmmanuel fulfills his calling, his teaching of the Truth, "there will be a time of many hundreds and, thus, two times a thousand years and more before the truth of the knowledge you brought among the people will be recognized and disseminated by a few human children."

According to Christian Frehner, the reference on page 104, verse 50, of "disseminated by a few human children" is defined as not only the Core Group of 49 at the Semjase Silver Star Center, but all those who have knowledge of the Truth and try living according to it (Frehner 2020, Email).

---

[196] Dr. V. Raghavan (no date, Document), "Ancient Sanskrit from India tell of UFO visit in 4,000 B.C.," Accessed January 25, 2020, http://veda.wikidot.com/ancient-sanskrit-from-india-tell-of-ufo-visit.

[197] Billy Meier, (2016, 104), *Talmud of Jmmanuel*, Landesgruppe, Canada.

We are witnessing that time presently because it is obvious that there have been two thousand years since the end of Jmmanuel's mission. In the present day and in "many hundreds of years to come," the "coming and going of aircraft and rockets" is happening with the space program at present. This is followed by the false teaching of the Truth by zealots. Next, the human aliens will reveal themselves in secrecy as Earth humans become knowing which will be followed by straying from the Truth and in turn threaten the universe with Earth humans acquired might. [198]

# Conclusion

Why do many people shy away from the Billy Meier account of humans from another planet coming to earth and enlightening us with the truth of life elsewhere in the universe, settlements and wars in the cosmos and in particular history regarding our own solar system and life immigrating to Earth?

One distinct answer is found in the difference in generations whereby the older generations are not as open to new information because they are more skeptical in their acceptance of new developments in space technology and space discoveries of extraterrestrial life.

A second observation is that those who are raised in a conservative Christian atmosphere tend to disagree with ufology even if they do agree that with all the stars in the sky there must be some that are habitable. This same group is also dead set on God being in charge of all things.

A third observation is that churches of all denominations do not want to touch the topic of alien life coming to Earth due to the fact that it will

---

[198] Brown, Lauretta, 2016. "Georgetown Study: Religion Worth $1.2 Trillion in U.S. Economy, More Than Google and Apple Combined." Accessed February 3, 2020. https://www.cnsnews.com/news/article/lauretta- brown/georgetown-study-religion-worth-12-trillion-us-economy- more-google-and.

*God, The Grandest Illusion*

drive people away from the church and it would upset their financial picture as well as destroy people's reliance on God.

As was pointed out earlier there is no God, but the fallout of such a revelation would impact every corner of religious belief and support. Here is the impact below.

1. Religious leaders would instantly be unemployed.
2. Religious places of worship would stand empty.
3. Religious publications of hymn books, evangelism media, Bibles, counseling material and any printed material in those or associated relevancy would come to a standstill.
4. Religious care facilities such as hospitals, retirement centers, and the like would cease religious services and remove icons of saints, crosses, etc. and appeal for secular support.
5. Religious outreach programs to the poor and needy, locally and overseas from natural disasters, war and underdeveloped countries would cease or change to secular support.
6. Religious TV, radio and internet programs would drop off the air.

Yes, at first it would be a big impact because religion is worth $1.2 trillion in US money according to a Georgetown Study. "The first estimate considered only the revenues of faith-based organizations, which came to $378 billion annually. The second estimate, $1.2 trillion, included the fair market value of goods and services provided by religious organizations and included contributions of businesses with religious roots. The third, higher-end, estimate of $4.8 trillion considers the household incomes of religiously affiliated Americans, assuming that they conduct their affairs according to their religious beliefs."

So, to prepare for the full "encounterance" of UFO visitation in years to come, as stated in the Talmud of Jmmanuel, the process must start now by introducing people to the reality of our ancestry from among the stars.

People have asked me "what about all the amazing things that God did as recorded in the Bible? The answer to the question is that UFO were part of that history as listed in several chapters that I dealt with earlier in this work. Other happenings with so-called miracles were events that took place with the natural movement of wind, storms, physics, nature and geological changes that occurred due to changes in the rotation and axis of the Earth that were the result of the Destroyer Comet as previously covered. There are natural disasters that occur from time to time that people label as signs of the end of the earth and other such blameworthlessness when really it is a matter of cause and effect of the science of our Earth and the Universe.

"God" believing religions have blocked our conscious- related advance for a social structure that is cognizant of rationality, logic and truth, national identity in history and present-day focus on our priorities of understanding ourselves, others and our Earth.

We have lost sight of the fact that of 102 passengers on the Mayflower, 41 of them were religious dissenters called Separatists who desired to worship the way that "they" wanted vs following the Church of England…the remaining were called "strangers" or non-believers by the Pilgrims. That comes out to 61 people (or rounded to 60% that preferred to have nothing to do with religion).

All three sources below confirm that there were two groups that fled England for Holland, https://www.crf- usa.org/foundations-of-our-constitution/mayflower- compact.html, https://ancestralfindings.com/mayflowerpassengers-not-religious-reasons/, and https://www.history.com/topics/colonial- america/mayflower-compact.

So right from the beginning **America was not founded on the leadership and rule of God**. The Mayflower Compact is only a testimony of the "religious" Separatists to follow an agreement <u>for the CIVILITY of life</u> between them and the non-believers, labeled as "strangers," and nothing else!

We know from previous testimony from the Plejaren that a God is none other than an ISHWISH, or in other words a King of Wisdom, and were the Kings that descended from the Cosmos as stated in the "Kings List" of extraterrestrial individuals who ruled in Sumerian times and up until approximately two-thousand years ago. (See the list of those that ruled per the chronological listing of "God" in this work).

Secondly, the **Pledge of Allegiance gives a false notion that America was founded "under God."** Congress ADDED the words "under God," due to the pressure from the Knights of Columbus in 1954, (*Gettysburg Flag Works*, https://www.gettysburgflag.com/history-of-the-pledge-of- allegiance).

Third, the **Constitution expressly guarantees the freedom of religious practices**, *Legal Information Institute*, https://www.law.cornell.edu/wex/free_exercise_clause. See also The Washington Post *"Should atheists who refuse to say 'so help men God' be excluded from the Air Force?* https://www.washingtonpost.com/news/volokh- conspiracy/wp/2014/09/08/should-atheists-who-refuse-to- say-so-help-me-god-be-excluded-from-the-air-force/.

Fourth, patriotic songs or expressions that incorporate God as the "blessing agent" for the United States is a further demonstration of the ignorance of individuals and institutions, religious, private or governmental, of the true history of our earth.

With all this said people still cling to their teddy bear of religion by singing "God Bless America" and reciting the "Pledge of Allegiance to the Flag" without a speck of knowledge of the extraterrestrial truth and influence of our past…but why? Because we are a people that like to have answers and there is a boat load of those that profess to have the answers and fire-off theories as if they are truth with no supporting data. Scientists refuse for the most part to get counsel from the contact reports of facts from the Plejaren that Billy Meier in Switzerland has documented since his first encounter in 1942 with a Plejaren.

*Dr. Ron Pleune*

Are you willing to put your name and reputation on the line as I have done through holding public meetings, handing out literature to people regarding the Billy Meier and the Plejaren, developing a website on Facebook and writing several books on the topic? I have seen their ships as well as other ships just 100 ft. from me…they are real, their technology is real, their history is real!!

Don't pull the covers over your head and refuse to listen to the truth that has been revealed in this work. Many people have gone with my wife and I "signaling for UFO" and witnessed their flying overhead as they signal back with their lights as an acknowledgement of our friendship. They heard the explanations from the Billy Meier story and have seen them with their eyes. Will you?

Space science questions it

Politicians poo-hoo it

Archeologists ignore it

Religionists reject it

The wise will learn from it…it's in plain sight!

Printed in the USA
CPSIA information can be obtained
at www.ICGtesting.com
LVHW012121041023
760082LV00003B/151